GOODBYE
UN-AMERICA

GOODBYE
UN-AMERICA

a novel by

JAMES ALDRIDGE

LITTLE, BROWN AND COMPANY   BOSTON   TORONTO

FIRST AMERICAN EDITION

205016

Library of Congress Cataloging in Publication Data

Aldridge, James.
  Goodbye un-America.

  I. Title.
PZ3.A3655Go 1979 [PR9619.3.A5] 823'.9'12 79-1029
ISBN 0-316-03114-3

BP

Published simultaneously in Canada
by Little, Brown & Company (Canada) Limited

PRINTED IN THE UNITED STATES OF AMERICA

GOODBYE
UN-AMERICA

CHAPTER

1

In the summer of 1955 I was living with my wife and two children at St Jean-Cap Ferrat in a decaying old villa called 'L'Escapade'. Up on the hill above us was Somerset Maugham's 'Mauresque', which overlooked the deep, blue bay of Villefranche, and from which the old master could see almost all the true Riviera as far west as Antibes. The other neighbour above us was one of the Rothschilds, whose villa had been turned into a sort of empty, marble museum of nineteenth-century objets d'art. At the foot of our mutual hill was St Jean itself, still a village then, although on one side of its bay was the huge 'Villa Singer' (Sinjay), and on the other side the rich old Bristol Hotel of Beaulieu.

It was an exotic and ridiculous setting for the peculiar drama that we played out on our verandahs and gardens and terraces that year. Drama is not a very good word any more. It was more of a confrontation. What else could you call a carefully prepared meeting between one of Roosevelt's advisers on Chinese affairs whose life had been devastated (like Alger Hiss's) by the condemnations of the Un-American Activities Committee, and his former friend who had actually denounced him to the committee and ruined him?

The idea of bringing the two men together again was so horrible and yet so fascinating that when it was first suggested I was repulsed and enthusiastic at the same time, because the events were still brutally fresh in 1955. Being

5

denounced as un-American was still a criminal condition, and people of my age don't have to be reminded of the savagery of those un-American years and of what happened to the people involved in them, particularly two men like Phillip Lovell, the victim, and Lester Terrada, his accuser. It was not the most famous case of its kind, not comparable with the Hiss-Chambers affair, but it was always a very special one because of the original intimacy and friendship of the two men, which ended in such hatred and finally in a sort of justice by tragedy.

I was only the consultant, not the originator of their meeting at Cap Ferrat. The woman who really fixed it was Dora Delorme, who also lived above us on the pine slopes of the Maugham-Rothschild hillside. Dora had once been the Paris buyer for the biggest department store in San Francisco, and later on had married one of the store's partners. She had inherited his wealth which had given her, in her late fifties, a fascination for the kind of political personalities that rich American women can indulge in.

As a young woman Dora had been a Venusian American beauty, but she was French by birth and French by a sort of peasant-property instinct which had brought her back to France in her sixties to live on land, not on money. She was fat, indulgent, arrogant, attractive, intelligent, violent and wicked. She came to me that hot July day in 1955 with her plan because Pip Lovell, the victim, was staying with us. Pip had not been imprisoned by a federal grand jury. Instead the Senate subcommittee had been content to brand him un-American and subversive, so that he had been ostracised, blacklisted, deprived of his passport and virtually exiled. It was so bad by 1952 that he had secretly left the United States and moved to France. Since then he had lived precariously in Paris among the dozens of other blacklisted Americans whose passports had been cancelled and whose livelihood had been taken away.

'Is your friend Lovell around anywhere?' Dora asked us when she drove up in her Peugeot and just sat there until we came out to her.

'No. He's in Nice with Monique,' I told her.

'Good,' she said. 'Then I'll get out.'

She pulled and pushed her bulk out of the car and walked up the path to a garden chair under its parasol. She dropped into it like an elephant flopping into a mud hole. We knew it must be something serious to persuade her to do that.

'Do get me a glass of something, Eileen,' she said sweetly to my wife.

She was always trying to break Eileen's deep wall of Irish suspicion, but she could never quiet manage it, and when Eileen went into the kitchen to get her something, Dora said: 'Can you imagine what I've come to ask you, Kit?'

'If it's one of your picnics,' I told her, 'it's out of the question.'

Dora laughed. She liked 'awful' Californian picnics, preferably in inaccessible places when her bulk suddenly ceased to be elephantine and she became instead a monumental sprite.

'It's nothing to do with a picnic,' she said.

'Then obviously it's something to do with Pip Lovell,' I said, 'and that's also out of the question.'

'Well . . .' she began tentatively.

'Leave him alone, Dora,' I told her. 'He's still too vulnerable to get involved with the kind of people you entertain up there.'

'What sort of people are you talking about?' she said innocently.

'The kind of people who would love to go back home to America and report secretly and fearfully that they had seen the notorious Phillip Lovell.'

'In my house?' she said indignantly. 'Think of the scandal. I'd be blacklisted.'

'You know very well that you don't care about the scandal,' I said.

It was true. Dora had a peculiar kind of courage that was not afraid of exposure to the still-scandalous presence of people like Pip Lovell. Most of his friends had long ago melted into the soupy mess of American fear, although not

7

all of them had deserted him. But Dora was not afraid to entertain him.

'There is a very good reason . . .' she said mysteriously.

'A good reason for what?'

'Why I want Lovell to come to dinner.'

Eileen had arrived with a glass of sirop de grenadine which Dora gulped down without a pause, but it was Eileen's suspicious Irish look that made Dora flutter a little.

'I never ever met Lovell,' Dora said, 'but I have known Lester Terrada for years.'

'That bastard,' I said vehemently.

'Don't be silly,' Dora said. 'You might as well call Banquo a bastard or Mercutio or any of those weird Shakespearean murderers.' Dora had a private store of Shakespeare characters, none of them right. 'Terrada is just as much a tragedy in this as Lovell is.'

'That's pretty silly,' I said. 'Terrada is the informer who ruined Pip and was made a hero for it. Some state or other even named a day after him.'

'Well, never mind all that,' Dora said impatiently. 'The point is that Terrada is coming down from Paris to stay with me for a few days, and he has asked me to invite Lovell over so that they can meet again. Wait . . .' she said, when I began to interrupt. 'He is actually coming down here expressly to see Lovell. He heard that Lovell was staying with you, and he asked me if I would invite him down here and then arrange the meeting.'

'You're mad,' Eileen said.

'You think so, pet?' Dora said appeasingly to her.

'What's the point in bringing them together again?' I said.

'No point at all,' she replied. 'Terrada simply asked me if I'd arrange it. So that's what I'm trying to do with your help. That's all.'

'No!' I said firmly.

'Why not?'

'Because it's a pretty horrible idea, and it won't do any-one any good.'

8

'How do you know it won't? Maybe your friend Lovell wants to see Terrada again.'

'I doubt it. In fact he may shoot Terrada on sight.'

'How do you know what he wants if you won't ask him?'

It was Eileen who said to me: 'Maybe she's right, Kit. Maybe Pip would enjoy a little revenge.'

But I still hesitated because it was all right for Eileen to think of revenge: she was a fighter and a savage who looked on everything as a contest of wills, whereas Pip Lovell was nothing if not civilised.

'Lovell's a full-grown man,' Dora insisted, 'so let him decide for himself.'

I thought about it, and about Pip whom I had known since 1941. And as if to widen the breach she had made in my defences Dora pressed on. 'It will be very discreet of course. Terrada himself doesn't want anyone to know about it.'

'I can imagine that,' I snarled.

Terrada was now a respectable, honourable, famous man, and the idea that he was dining and talking to the traitor he had exposed would, at that time, have done him considerable damage. Unless, of course, it was some sort of a trap. But I dismissed that idea. Too obvious.

'Terrada says he knew you well in New York in 1941,' Dora said enticingly.

'I knew them both in 1941. They were very close friends then.'

'Then let them get at each other again,' Dora said.

By now my reasoning had come around to hers. 'All right,' I agreed. 'At least I'll put it to Pip and that's all I'll do.'

Dora got up. Business done, no need to sit around. When she got back into her Peugeot you could hear the shock absorbers sink.

'Terrada will arrive on Sunday with his wife and son.'

'His wife and son!' I said stupidly. 'Don't you know that Terrada's wife was once Pip's wife? And that their son is really Pip's son?'

'I knew about the wife, but not about the son,' she said. And suddenly she laughed heartily from her fat white throat. 'What silly fools we mortals be,' she said and took off noisily before I could change my mind.

As we watched the gravel settle down Eileen said, 'I think if I were Pip I'd poison the both of them.'

I kissed my fighting wife. I was still in some doubt about the whole idea, and I thought I'd better sit down and think about it before I actually told Pip. I had to think about Pip himself, about his ex-wife Judy, his son, and the ten years of Pip's life as an exile and a 'traitor'. And no matter what way I thought of it I knew that any meeting with Terrada was hardly going to be fair on Pip because he was still the outcast on the bottom, while Terrada was very much the hero on the top. On the other hand would a meeting be so bad? I had to think carefully about the two men I had known in that New York winter of 1941 when I had briefly and ineffectually worked for *Time* and *Life* with Phillip Lovell and Lester Terrada as my office companions and American friends.

2

I had gone to work for *Time* and *Life* in 1941 because I had been in the Finnish and Norwegian and Greek and Western Desert wars, so they offered me a job as one of their war correspondents providing I spent three or four months on *Time* in New York learning their techniques. I joined their World War section which was edited then by Charles Wertenbaker and John Hersey, and I was given a desk in a corner office which had a thick carpet on the floor and stuffed birds on the walls. The office had previously belonged to John Stuart Martin, the one-armed former editor of *Time*, who was no longer editor, but whose feathery ghosts had remained behind him on our neat grey walls.

I shared the office with Teddy (Theodore H.) White and an Oklahoman called Sam Salt who was one of those American newspapermen you remember all your life with affection and regret that you didn't know him longer and better. On one side of our corner was Wert's office, and along a length of aseptic corridor on the other side was room after room of girl researchers. Then there was Hersey's office, and finally the room shared by Pip Lovell and Lester Terrada.

That corner of the 29th floor was a good place to be that winter and spring, because there was plenty of talent and good company and good talk. Hersey was young and clever, and far too good for the place. So was Teddy White. Above all, so was Wertenbaker, who was the prince we served so gladly. It was Wert who gave us our liberties and tolerated our indulgences and encouraged our talents, whatever they were. Perhaps Luce, who ran *Time* and *Life*, knew what he had in Wertenbaker, and perhaps that corner of the 29th floor was one of Luce's real achievements.

Teddy, then, was writing a book about Chiang Kai-shek (he had just come back from China). I was writing a novel about the Greek war, and Sam was obligingly Sam. Sam read the funnies, chuckled, tickled his big nose, and breakfasted every morning on bourbon from a bottle in his bottom drawer and a carton of milk brought in by one of the office boys. When all the youth and industry and ambition of Teddy and myself got too much for Sam, he would stretch his arms and say:

'Well, you guys, something has to be done for your morale.'

So Sam would suggest, or rather insist, that we all take a trip on the Staten Island ferry to see the Statue of Liberty under 'the best possible conditions'. For Sam that meant a cold, miserable and foggy day when we would huddle up the front of the deserted ferry, wrapped in our overcoats, staring wet-faced through the fog and the gloom, and taking very long swigs of life from the bottle of bourbon that Sam had brought with him in his overcoat pocket. Sam knew what he was doing, and those sentimental journeys had nothing to do with the Statue of Liberty which Sam never looked at.

We were not, of course, serious drinking men, but Sam thought it would do me good to see other aspects of America under 'the best possible conditions', so our depredations into *Time*'s office hours became a bit too much, and someone upstairs decided to break us up. Wert was overruled, and I was shifted out of the office. I was obviously the chief corrupter. I was a bird of passage, a foreigner, a fascinated observer and lover of New York, and I had no taste for writing about war from the 29th floor.

I was therefore sent down the corridor to share the room that Lovell and Terrada worked in, where there was no Sam to encourage me in my private Americanisms. Actually, it seemed an odd thing to do because Lovell and Terrada were always off on their own somewhere. In the old corner office John Hersey had dropped in on our club to gossip with Teddy and Sam and me, and Wert himself liked to look in and swap stories. But in this office Lovell and Terrada kept to themselves. There was obviously nothing physical in it, but there was something else, something that was total and effective and so preoccupying for them that they had become inseparables, and Sam said to me when I was shifted:

'You're in interesting American country down there, Kit, so watch yourself.'

From the outset it was clear that it was Terrada who was the stronger character of the two. He was a big, solid man, with thick legs, abundant hair and a wide forehead. He was quick, erudite, stubborn, and he had (to my foreign ear) a sort of biblical prophetic air about him. He was one of the stout prophets, not one of the thin ones. One of the strong ones, too, not one of the hesitant ones. He spoke always as if he expected you to understand that his prophetic reasoning should be listened to; but for some inexplicable reason I always thought of him as a one generation man, as if there was nothing before him, and there would be nothing after him. His father had been a Bohemian glass-blower, his mother a starving Pole from Tilsit, and he had invented his own name from something originally Czech. But he seemed to breathe the American air as if the rest of the nation was breathing with him.

Pip, on the other hand, seemed to be a light-weight and transparent aristocrat from New England. He was a cheerful man, a little too much, perhaps, as if he were ashamed of something, or hiding some sort of failing. But he had something very old in him as well, as if he had been thinned out too much (like his name) by the explosion of American life into cities and blast furnaces and mine-pits.

'You're right, you're right, you're right,' he would say to Terrada as they argued some point of ideological impor-

13

tance concerning the Atlanta Constitution, the Mayflower Compact, the Pewter Muggers – anything that flowered from the bloom of the American existence.

What Pip always seemed to be doing was handing America over to Terrada, as if that was the right thing for him to do. As if he, personally, had no more claim left on the Republic. It took me a little while to understand what Pip really meant, and to appreciate what he was trying to do. But once I did grasp it, my respect for the man became considerable, and my affection for his America became profound.

In fact, what I did manage to discover, quite quickly, was that Pip was not in the same category as Terrada. The two men were really arguing rather than discussing. They were at opposite ends of something, rather than men on the same side. They were attached yet divided.

But by what?

I thought (stupidly) at first that it was one of the senior girl researchers, Judy Jamieson, who would appear sometimes in our corridor and lean in our doorway and talk to all three of us. She was really talking to the other two, not to me. In fact she was talking to only one of them. But to which one? Judy Jamieson was not exactly a pretty girl, and she had an awkward little laugh. But she was a fairly high-born, well-groomed girl, a tidy and organised girl with neat dark hair, a faint smile, a sure-fire mouth and very attractive teeth and skin. Judy looked like a Baltimore belle who had organised her appearance rather than having been born with it. That was the time of pearl necklaces and angora sweaters and sensible skirts, and that was what suited Judy best. But sometimes she would rattle a pencil between the perfect teeth of her slightly opened mouth, and it was so strangely, sexually enticing that I realised it was part of an instinctive sexual attack by a girl who knew that she had to use ankles and wrists and devices, rather than figure and flesh. And it was very effective.

One day Judy leaned on our doorway and said, 'Will you come to dinner at my place on Thursday?'

I looked up but didn't reply. She didn't mean me. The other two didn't reply either.

'I mean you, Kit,' she said determinedly, as if it had to be done.

'Me?'

'Don't, for heaven's sake, speak in echoes,' she said. 'Of course I mean you.'

I was flattered, and I said instantly I would be there. 'Eight o'clock,' she said, and gave me a little card with her Greenwich Village address on it.

That was all. I didn't look at the other two because I knew that Judy really wanted one of them, not me, and I was laughing to myself wondering how she was going to use me as an implement for her choice because that seemed to be the only reason why she should invite me.

'Great stuff, Kit,' Pip said to me, his eyes laughing.

'This bloody Englishman comes in here and steals our girl from right under our noses,' Terrada said in his big way, trying to take-off my English accent.

In fact Judy in her neat apartment with a 'coloured' maid (Judy had money of her own and it was 1941) was something different from the Judy of our corridors. She was a little embarrassed in a superior sort of way, and I realised in fact how like Pip she was. She looked a little like him. She had the same embarrassed laugh, and the same too-smiling eyes. She was more of the intellectual than Pip, but if you'd put a grey flannel suit on her she would have passed for Pip's neater brother. Superficially, they were built for each other except that Judy was made of iron whereas Pip was nearer the bronze age.

'Why did you ask me to dinner?' I said to her over the oysters.

'Because those two get on my nerves sometimes,' she said, like a small dog growling over a bone. 'What on earth do they talk about all the time?'

I had not asked myself that question, but when I thought about it the real answer suddenly came to me.

'America,' I said.

15

She looked surprised but then she laughed. 'Of course!'

'In fact it just occurred to me,' I said.

'So they're having an affair with the nation,' she said sarcastically. 'No wonder they don't see anybody else.'

That was about all that ever came of that neat, gracious, napkined dinner. But I walked most of the way home to the old Murray Hill Hotel (where I was living) wondering which man Judy really wanted. I was pretty sure it was Pip, only I wasn't sure that Pip wanted her. There had always been a lot of sexual talk about women (particularly the researchers) in those neat little *Time* boxes on the 29th floor, and none of the talk was suitable for marriage. But after that dinner with Judy I began to watch Pip and Terrada closely, and it was clear that Judy's door-leaning sessions had both men very interested because they never mentioned her when they started to relish the meat and flesh of the other girls. Within a week Terrada was invited to dinner, and a few days later, Pip. So I had been the formal opening, the respectable stepping-stone for Judy's maidenly ambitions. But I had to laugh at the weird ritual of it. Judy was a very respectable and conventional girl, and I think that was actually what attracted both men to her.

But she was not, as I had suspected, the thing that divided them. I had thought so briefly because I was then so ignorant of America itself. I had simply missed the real nuances of Pip and Terrada's subtle disagreements because I didn't know enough American social philosophy, American history, American ideology. Only after I had listened to a particularly long argument they had about Parrington's book *Main Currents in American Thought* did I finally begin to detect the nature of their real disagreement. But I had to question Pip closely before I eventually got a clue to it as well as a clue to Pip himself.

Despite his Waspish upbringing in the puritanism and liberalism of eighteenth-century colonial democracy (he was a descendant of James Lovell) Pip was out of love with his own inheritance. The historical measure of the underlying ideology of the American intellectual attitudes of 1941

16

was the Jackson-Jeffersonian frontier democracy, but Pip, who had more right than most to feel that this was a personal tradition, rejected it outright. I don't mean that he chose Marxism or some other universal ideology. He knew little or nothing about Marxism, and wasn't even interested in it. Pip was a purely American thinker, and he put his view to me very simply one day as we sat eating lunch (Terrada had gone to Washington for the day) in the underground restaurant where you could watch the girl skaters zooming around the sunken garden of Rockefeller Center.

'America,' he said, 'is continually trying to re-create itself in the frontier image of the hardy individual and the honest pioneer farmer – the open sort of freedom that space and wilderness could give to those men. But it's all quite stupid now,' he said, 'because America is really a nation of urban peasant immigration from Europe, and our practical philosophy ought to begin there.'

I protested that not all immigration had been peasantry from Europe.

'After 1870,' he said, 'all immigration, the great bulk of our population, came directly from European peasant stock; or they were European artisans who were themselves of peasant stock. Modern America was built and populated by the landless peasantry and the urbanised poor of Europe.'

'So?'

'You see, Kit, they came here with European peasant mentality. What were they hungry for? Material acquisition, for instance, is built into the peasant. So is vulgarity. So is naturalism in all things. So is inventiveness and health and quick passion and guts. So is violence and superstition and sentimentality, as well as a powerful material and religious conservatism and an almost brutal self-interest. And that's exactly where modern America begins. That's the real raw material we are dealing with. Not the neat-minded frontiersman with flint-lock and self-sufficient farmlands and endless horizons over the hill. That sort of stuff is only a dangerous deception now, a myth, and you

17

can't tack it on to the tail of a peasant without doing both a lot of damage.'

When I protested again that surely he was being harsh, that surely the original frontier-minded Constitution and the Bill of Rights were still important, he said with an irritable little shrug: 'Of course they're important. I'm not denying them. But at best they're only a juridical safeguard. Jefferson himself said: "No society can make a perpetual Constitution, or even a perpetual law." The Constitution was merely a great outline for essential safeguards of the time. So are the amendments. That's all they are supposed to be. For the rest, the social philosophy of the United States ought to begin all over again with our peasant and urban immigration. Start there and build on that.'

'But surely the old philosophy is the best basis you've got?'

We downed another crystalline martini and Pip said, 'How can you say that? What possible link, for instance, has a Swabian peasant who becomes a Pittsburgh steel puddler got with all the Jeffersonian and Jacksonian traditions? None. What right has a Ukrainian mujik or a Polish Jew or an Irish potato-farmer or a Scottish crofter got to feel that Nathaniel Hawthorne is his spiritual and cultural antecedent? Absolutely none! It's ridiculous. There is absolutely no connection.'

'But aren't you being a bit patrician about all this?' I said. 'Aren't you denying to the immigrants something that you were fortunate enough to be born into?'

'No! No! No!' he said angrily, as one of the Rockefeller girls splashed our window with her soggy ice. 'Personally, I don't want the damned birthright, or the tradition. I've abandoned it. In fact I'm trying to tell the first generation of our urban peasantry that this is their country, that our real philosophy must begin with them and what they've brought with them, not with what's left of me. They're being tricked.'

I still felt a bit sarcastic and I said: 'You mean they should start with their acquisitiveness, meanness and vulgarity?'

'Oh, come off it, Kit,' he said. 'I don't mean that's what they should live by. On the contrary, that's what they ought to abandon. I simply want them to understand what *is*. What they've brought with them. Then they can change it if they want to, for whatever they think is better. That's all.'

'So you want to abandon the tradition entirely?'

'More or less.'

'You want your urban peasants to reshape themselves in another way?'

'Yes.'

'Which way?'

'Oh Christ, I don't know that, Kit. Nobody does. That's where we have to begin. But it can only be an American way, because there's no other criterion for our situation.'

'You know, you're denying a marvellous thing,' I suggested.

'Of course,' he said resignedly. 'But I'm only denying something that is lost and gone for ever. I want this nation to get away from its dying myths and rebuild itself from all this marvellous stuff that bursts with vulgar energy and almost bestial passion. I don't exactly fit into it personally, but I'll live with it gladly and count myself part of it, and I'll go where it goes. That's all it is, Kit. Nothing special, really.'

Nothing special.

I knew it was something very special, because it uprooted the old American view of itself. I realised then what all those arguments with Terrada were really about, and what was their real division. They were literally poles apart. Pip, the pre-1840 aristocrat and freeholder, was throwing in his lot with the huddled masses at the foot of the Statue of Liberty, whereas Terrada the immigrant was a passionate prophet of the squirearchy of 1776 and the great American tradition, so that almost everything they said to each other about American ethics and morals and culture was determined by their vastly different American attitudes.

A hopeless situation; maybe a dangerous one in this

19

forever self-inventing country, wherein such arguments were the root of that extraordinary thing they called Americanism. No wonder Judy was jealous of America, no wonder she had difficulty making up her mind which one of them she wanted, because she was as deep in the confusion of being an American as they were.

CHAPTER
3

It went on like that between them all winter. Every subject that touched on their different Americas involved their different ideologies. I never heard them talk very seriously of other subjects. I never heard them import any dangerous philosophies into it. That was curious, because after all Terrada was one of the department's experts on Russia (he had lived there for two years), and Pip was our expert on China (he had been brought up in China by his missionary parents and spoke Chinese).

But I remember the first time their disagreement touched on something outside their usual historical confrontations. Once a week the department had a conference with Henry Luce himself. I did not attend these meetings because they were policy briefings, and I certainly had nothing to do with policy making. But Wert took me into one of them to give me the feel of the place.

It was really an embarrassment because they all called Luce 'Harry' and the air was thick with editorial democracy in which I detected the normal editorial autocracy. Luce was the policy. But we did discuss, and I must say that Luce listened attentively. This particular day the discussion was on *Time*'s policy towards Russia at war. Roosevelt had just agreed to let the battered Russians have a few trucks and some Airacobra fighter planes, but Luce opposed this because he opposed Roosevelt, and *Time* then was more pro-German than pro-Russian. In the editorial 'debate' Terrada suggested that America should confine its help to sending Russia bandages and used clothes and some surplus dried milk powder. Luce agreed.

But I heard Pip laugh. 'Listen, Harry,' he said. 'Inside six months the Japanese will probably attack us. Inside two years we will be fighting Germans in Europe. So who are we fooling if we only give the Russians old clothes and dirty bandages?'

'That's just speculation, Pip,' Luce said.

'No, it isn't. The more Germans the Russians kill now the better it will be for our boys when they have to start killing Germans. Nothing speculative in that.'

I wasn't asked for my opinion, and I didn't offer it. But that seemed like a sensible anticipation to me, although I wasn't so sure that Japan was going to attack the United States. In fact I thought it impossible.

But Pip understood China and Japan the same way that he understood the United States. He never looked at Asian countries with American eyes. He understood them with their own eyes. But I remember also being impressed that day with Terrada's large and articulate prophecies about the war in Europe. The Russians, Terrada said, were undoubtedly retreating clean out of Europe, and they would hide themselves in the vast wastes of Siberia where they would conduct a grim, primitive thirty-year war against the Germans, who would successfully occupy all European Russia inside two months. It was a common enough prediction by experts at the time, but the only man there who seemed to be arguing silently with his face and eyes and amused lips, was Pip. He knew Terrada was wrong, but he didn't bother to argue. He wasn't very interested.

I asked Wert after this conference why Luce kept Pip Lovell on, since he was obviously something of a discord in the chicken coop.

'Don't be hard on Harry,' Wert said loyally. 'He and Pip were boys in China together, and they're old friends.'

'That's not the reason,' I said.

Wert laughed. 'No it isn't,' he said. 'Pip has a genius for

knowing what *is*. That makes him too valuable for a news magazine like ours to do without.'

'What about Terrada?'

'Now don't start consulting me about friends and enemies,' Wert said, but he added: 'Terrada is the sort of American who actually admires the magazine, and that's what makes him so valuable.'

'You mean Pip doesn't care a damn about it?'

'I didn't say that. But what are you getting at anyway?'

'Nothing,' I said. 'I just want to know what makes them such good friends.'

Wert had been watching me to see if my motives were pure and simple. He leaned back in his metal chair and chewed on his little black New Orleans cheroot and said: 'You'd have to know a lot more about America to appreciate the real fascination of that friendship.'

'Is it that complicated?'

'I guess it is. Americans have a curious inbuilt role that they all play as citizens of our free republic, Kit. We do it without thinking about it. We're always looking at the kind of America we're living in, and the kind of American the other guy is. So when you get that on an intellectual level it develops a sort of moral responsibility to justify yourself as an American. Somewhere in all this, if you look hard enough, you'll find the curious mess those two are in.'

'Maybe it's more mess than friendship,' I suggested.

Wert turned his back on me and put his feet on the window sill. 'Now you're digging a bit too deep. Why don't you ask Pip or Lester what you want to know?'

'Because I don't know what it is I want to know,' I said, 'and I can't help being curious about them.'

Wert didn't like any of it but I think he was as interested in them or as curious as I was, so he thought for a moment and said: 'All right, I'll give you one more clue, just one, and after that you're on you're own. Pip, being a Lovell, went to Groton and Yale and sailed through it all without having to think about it. But Terrada had to grub his way by God-knows-what effort of will and sacrifice to get to Harvard, where he was probably the best undergraduate student they've ever had in the history of the Americas. Brilliant! And he did it with holes in his shoes and no tails on his shirts because his sister kept cutting them off to remake the worn collars.'

'But that sort of difference could happen anywhere.'

'Maybe. But when it happens in the United States it represents what you think of yourself for the rest of your life as well as what happens to you. When Pip graduated he wanted to go back to China so he just walked into one of the half-dozen U.S. foundations that operate in China and that was all he had to do, even though we were still in the tail end of the Depression. But look what happened to Terrada. He wanted a job as a newspaperman but he couldn't even get in the door. That's why he went to Russia on some godawful grain ship that nearly killed him.'

'Was he a communist?'

'I suppose he was. He wanted to see the great experiment. He could already speak Russian because they spoke nothing but Slovak at home, and it wasn't much of a step to Russian. He got a job in Moscow in some sort of travel agency, and on the side he started feeding one of the AP or UP guys bits of information and eventually they made him a sort of stringer. After a couple of years he came back to the U.S. and wrote that book which demolished the great experiment, and he's never looked back. But it was all uphill for Lester, and when you put a guy like Lester into the same balloon with Pip Lovell you get what you've got . . . the American osmosis at work.'

I was only partly satisfied. 'But they've got nothing in common, and you still haven't explained how they manage to overcome that.'.

Wert got up and looked out of the window at the first snowflakes of the day falling on the very tip of the spire of the Collegiate Church of St Nicholas, which was right underneath us. Wert had a slouching sort of shrug that somehow matched his moustache and his way of talking. 'I've been trying to tell you,' he said, 'that the only thing Pip and Terrada have in common is that they're both American, but you don't seem to be listening.' He held up his hand to stop a further question. 'And that's all I'm telling you, Kit. If you want to know anything more you'll have to work backwards from that.'

If I had been doing a serious research into their lives I would have done just that – worked backwards. But I wasn't that serious. In fact I was far more intrigued by Judy at the time; or rather it was the peculiar triangle she was making that added another dimension to the friendship.

I suppose I should have realised from the outset which one of the two men she was trying to impress, but I still didn't know enough about them, and it was only later that it all became clear. Judy had a rich aunt with a country house in Ridgeford, Connecticut, and Judy stood in our office doorway one Wednesday morning and invited us all up there for the November weekend. There was only a moment's hesitation before we all accepted, so on the Friday we all drove up to Connecticut in Judy's Ford.

There were in fact two houses, one for Aunt Felice who wasn't there, and the other for her guests. Both houses looked as if they had historical family connections with the district, but as Pip said many years later when I reminded him of those beautiful farmhouses and their atmosphere: 'All bought with money.' Even so it was fairly discreet money, although I was impressed with the private petrol pump near the big stables. You just pumped the gas out as if it came straight from the earth.

Neither Pip nor Terrada could ride but I could, and while the others sat around the fire in those comfortable living rooms attended by a black butler and his wife, I followed the bridle paths worn by a hundred guests before me all over those private Connecticut hills, brushed loftily with thin snow so that they were cold without being bare, white without being buried. I got back at five o'clock, had a hot shower, and found the others drinking martinis and waiting for me because we were to drive across the hillsides to the house of Marin Poplar, one of America's most famous

25

columnists. It was only when we were on the way over the narrow country roads in Aunt Felice's large Packard, driven by the petite Judy, that Pip whispered to me:

'It's America-First country up here, Kit, so watch yourself. This guy Poplar doesn't like the British and he hates Roosevelt and the unions, so you'd better know what you're talking about if you get into any argument about anything political.'

'I never argue about anything political,' I told him.

'You may have to,' he said.

Marin Poplar's house was another old Connecticut farmhouse with a barn attached to it, and one of the first things Mrs Poplar did was to take the three of us (not Judy) to the big white barn and show us the old storage landing which was furnished with desks, filing cabinets, typewriters, a telex, a large fan, and a soft felt carpet.

'This is where he works,' Mrs Poplar said in an almost hushed voice.

I was about to ask 'Where who works?' when Pip said: 'Well I'll be damned,' and I recognised one of his drier comments.

The entire carpeted floor of the barn, fully fifty feet long and thirty wide, was covered in neat rows of files; streets of them, probably several hundred in all, and the first file I looked at read: 'Brdgs, H4 Extradition.'

'So that's his system,' Terrada said in his impressive voice.

'Not everyone is allowed up here,' Mrs Poplar said to Terrada, 'but we thought you'd be interested.'

'I am,' Terrada said, very impressed, and Pip would tell me later that he saw the names of almost every union leader in the United States and all the most important figures in the Roosevelt administration as he walked along those neat little avenues of files.

We waited for Pip to come back from his exploration (Terrada and I didn't dare) and then we were taken back into the house through a little alcove where Marin Poplar was stirring martinis with a long glass spoon in a large glass jug.

'Mama, your pants are showing,' he said to his plump and pleasant wife who was always a little breathless.

Mrs Poplar looked over her shoulder at her dress. We all looked over her shoulder. An inch of her slip was showing, so she straightened her jersey dress and took us in to meet the other guests who were being looked after by the Poplars' daughter and Judy.

Though I knew what America First did and said and thought, I knew too little about American politics to be impressed then with the names I heard that day: Keyes Sanford, a famous corporation lawyer, Robert Bannerman of Bannerman & Bruce the advertising agency, and a young man called Moran who looked like a college student but who was already a well-known attorney. I have almost nothing to say about Moran because I can't quite remember him, but Sanford and Bannerman looked like elderly, settled, successful, unhappy American businessmen. They never raised their voices and they behaved impeccably as far as I, the young English stranger, was concerned. So I judged them as I saw them.

Keyes Sanford, the lawyer, had once been the liberal governor of one of the New England states and had been a supporter of Governor Franklin D. Roosevelt of New York when Hoover was President. But Sanford now despised Roosevelt and he was considered a tragic figure because he had a throat disease and was slowly losing his voice. He spoke a little above a whisper. Bannerman was also considered a sad man because his only son had committed suicide by jumping out of a small plane without a parachute. But unlike Sanford, Bannerman had been a Republican all his life, and what was intriguing about him was the famous advertising campaign he had launched in the early thirties to persuade Americans that certain American historical figures were the reincarnation of the apostles and the disciples, among them Thomas Jefferson (Mark), Washington (Matthew), Alexander Hamilton (Luke), and Robert E. Lee (John). James Gordon Bennet was St Paul and Thomas Edison was Peter. In addition the disciples would reappear

27

again and again in later disguises. William Jennings Bryan, for instance, would appear as St Paul – or the other way round.

I couldn't believe that Bannerman had launched his campaign with anything but tongue in cheek, but Pip insisted that you had to take him seriously and said that Bannerman was as serious about his apostles as Bruce Barton was about Christ when he wrote his book called *The Man Nobody Knows*, describing Jesus as the founder of modern business because he had picked up twelve men from the bottom ranks of business and forged them into an organisation that conquered the world.

I can hardly remember those men – those quiet, throatless men, and I can't remember their wives at all. But after that November night I always considered those Connecticut hillsides to be 'Terrada country' because it was obvious that these men were pleased to meet Terrada and wanted to listen to him and talk to him. It became Terrada's night, which is how Judy had planned it. She sat back in a big chintz chair and watched Terrada's performance – the reformed communist, the exposer of the great experiment. She had a kittenish smile as that Old Testament voice told them what was right and wrong with the world – I mean politically not morally.

Naturally it was America they also talked about, though in courtesy and deference to me, an Englishman, not the America of America First and Colonel Lindbergh – their America – but the America of Thorstein Veblen whose book *The Theory of the Leisure Class* had persuaded earlier Americans that the great nineteenth-century robber barons of railroad, real estate, mines and stock exchange were fulfilling their symbolic class status and doing their country a service by their conspicuous and vulgar consumption of wealth.

Terrada, eyes unfocussed, said that America would always be able to absorb every kind of excess as well as every kind of poverty, because the real issue was not what an individual did with his money but whether in wasting it he

28

infringed the rights of others. Consumption, however conspicuous, could never be an infringement on the individual in a free society where the poor man had exactly the same rights as a rich one. Then Sandford quoted, in a whisper, the San Mateo County Case of 1905 to show that there was a constitutional reason for limiting the power of any government to interfere in business, but when we sat down to a very gracious dinner on a polished table with candles and silver and crystal goblets Pip said:

'Well, personally I always thought that that thief Jay Gould was the logical outcome of Jackson and Jefferson, and now you've all proved it.' It was one of the remarks Terrada would later use to condemn him with.

I don't remember anything more about that dinner because we all drank too much wine which blurred the men and the women and the politics and left us all naked with our own personalities to think about. But it had given another twist to the extraordinary way these two men survived their obvious differences.

There was more to come although it happened in a round-about way. Judy had a cousin called Aimee who was, she said, half-horse and half-woman. That is, Aimee said so herself. In fact she was half-girl half-woman – the orphaned daughter of another aunt and her husband who had been killed in a freak rock fall in the Redmond National Park. On the Sunday, when it was already snowing rather thick and wild outside, Aimee persuaded me to help her carry half a dozen buckets of warm mash from Aunt Felice's kitchen to the stables behind the house.

As we poured the mash into the feed troughs for the three horses Aimee said: 'What on earth were Pip and Lester arguing about all last night?'

'I haven't the foggiest idea,' I said. 'I didn't even know they were arguing.'

'They sat up half the night talking downstairs, and it must have been something serious because they didn't let up until three in the morning.'

'Oh, that's normal for those two,' I said.

'Do they always argue like that?'

'Most of the time.'

'How do they remain such good friends then?'

'Ah . . .' I said as I poured a bucket of mash into a trough with 'Beauty' burned into it. 'That's the million-dollar mystery, Aimee.'

'If it stops snowing I'll take you out this afternoon,' she said as she carelessly slopped some mash over my foot. 'Have you ever ridden in the snow?'

'Never. Not in deep snow.'

'Well I'll tell you, Kit,' she said with her half-horse showing. 'The first thing you've got to remember is to forget yourself and think of the horse's legs. They have to lift their legs high in the snow, and you've got to move with them. It's all rhythm, otherwise they break their legs.'

'What was Judy doing when they were arguing?' I asked her.

'Just sitting there listening, I guess,' she said. 'Which one do you think Judy's going to end up with?'

'Is she trying to end up with one of them?'

'As if you didn't know!' Aimee said with a nudge that bruised my ribs.

'If you were Judy which one would you choose?' I asked her, rubbing my ribs.

Aimee was ready to bounce and longing to be teased. 'They're much too old for me,' she said contemptuously. 'I hate old men. Anyway, they'll probably end up shooting each other. Like this.'

She threw a spoonful of warm mash and hit me on the chest. Aimee was now dying for a fight, and because I was twenty-three and feeling fatherly and obliging I replied with a spoonful of the mash which hit Aimee on the neck. She yelped like a flop-eared puppy and plucked a handful of the stuff from one of the troughs and shot it at my head. I ducked. It hit the side of one of the stalls. I replied with a handful which hit Aimee on the right breast, and when she missed me again we began a serious mash fight which only ended when the horses began to get some of it and started

30

kicking and complaining. So we moved outside to continue it with snow, and by now Aimee was in ecstasies.

'Wait, Kit, wait . . .' she shouted as I raised a hand with a very large ball of snow in it. 'Don't you just wish everything could just stand still right now, like this, forever?'

Yes, I said, I wished it could.

She stood in the snow in her half boots and torn jeans and poured a snowball down my neck as we plunged into the fight again, which we continued until we were both hot and exhausted.

'Oh my God . . . . Forever and forever and forever!' she said happily and fell back into a big bank of snow in a palmy euphoria.

I had had enough, but just as we were about to go inside, Lester Terrada appeared at the side door of the house and stood there for a moment looking at the dark sky. I didn't realise what Aimee was doing, but then I saw her pull a handful of the compacted mash out of her jacket pocket (she had been saving it for me) and before Terrada could duck she hit him square on the side of the face with it. It was soft stuff and didn't hurt, and I thought Terrada would simply bend down and reply with a well-packed snowball.

'You should have ducked,' Aimee shouted, preparing for another fight.

But Terrada was stunned, in fact shocked, hurt and overcome. I don't know whether he resembled more a pudgy little boy who had been slapped by a bully, or a harmless innocent who had just been hit with some awful injustice which he didn't understand.

'Cut that out, Aimee.' It was Pip, tapping angrily at the window.

A snowball hit the window and Pip emerged like a schoolboy and pushed Aimee into the snow. It was still a game, but Terrada, eyes unseeing, slowly wiped the mash from his face with a handkerchief and went inside.

'What's the matter with him?' Aimee said as she went on pelting Pip with snowballs.

31

'Leave him alone,' Pip said, as he returned the bombardment. 'He's not the type for this sort of thing.'

'Bullshit!' Aimee said.

We forgave Aimee because she loved horses and had just come through the rigours of Bryn Mawr.

'I mean it, Aimee,' Pip said. 'Don't tease him. He doesn't understand.'

Aimee went back to her horses in disgust. Half an hour later I heard Judy quarrelling with her in the kitchen and I leaned against the window and listened to them.

'Pip was right,' Judy was saying in her neat, vigorous way. 'You just don't do that sort of thing to Lester.'

'Why? What's so special about him?' Aimee said brazenly.

'Nothing at all. But you ought to show him a little more respect. That's all I'm saying to you. So pay attention.'

'What about the others?' Aimee said. 'They didn't mind.'

'They're quite different. Lester's vulnerable, and you were behaving like a vulgar little rich kid pelting an old man.'

'Oh for Christ's sake,' Aimee complained. 'I know he's old, but he's not that old. Kit's English, and he didn't mind.'

'I don't care about the others,' Judy said stubbornly. 'I'm responsible for Lester, and I won't have him embarrassed. It was unpardonable.'

'Okay, it was unpardonable,' Aimee said with a shrug. 'So you know what you can do with Lester Terrada.'

'Don't be vulgar!'

'Are you going to marry him?'

'Oh, for heaven's sake shut up.'

I walked away, and because there was nothing else to do with that early snowstorm blotting out road, hedge and bridle path, I dug myself into a couch and began to read one of Aimee's books, *Leonardo da Vinci and the Horse*. For the rest of the morning we all sat around reading, except Terrada, who was so upset that he had gone back to bed.

'He's all right,' Pip explained to Judy. 'He needs a little time to get over it, that's all.'

'Damn that girl.'

Pip laughed. 'Lester never knows what hits him until it hits him; then he takes a little while to think it out. He'll be down this afternoon.'

Terrada eventually came down for lunch, and both Judy and Pip treated him like a wounded bird in need of care and protection. Judy mothered him and respected him and behaved apologetically, and Pip jollied him and was so normal that he was a little too normal. I felt I had to do the same until Aimee couldn't stand it any longer. She nudged me on the couch and said in a loud whisper:

'I can't stand this. Come on out and I'll show you how to ride in snow.'

'Okay.'

I followed her to the stables, and after we had rubbed down the two horses we saddled them and I followed Aimee out through the yard and along the gravel roadway until we came to a gate which we had to dig open. We were then face to face with an empty field and Aimee looked up at the perfect white slope, blue with snow, and she sighed like a child. 'My God. What they're missing,' she said.

'What who's missing?'

She nodded backwards at the house. 'Them!' she said. 'They're comic.'

'Who?' I teased.

'Those three. That little *ménage à trois*.'

She bit her fingernails as she blew on her cold hands, and with her eyes narrowed and her feet ready to dig into her horse she said into the middle distance: 'The thing is that Pip is a Lovell whereas Terrada is a very common man and never the twain shall meet. Let's go . . . .' She dug her heels into the flanks and shouted, 'Watch my legs and do what I do.'

I did what Aimee did for the next two hours and it was only that night as I lay in bed that I realised what hard work it had been keeping in rhythm with those four, hot, horse

33

legs rising and falling like muscular pistons. I could hardly move and I fell asleep the moment my head hit the pillow.

I was awakened in the middle of the night by Aimee in pyjamas. 'Shhh!' she said, sitting on my bed as I sat up. 'It's me.'

'What's the matter?'

'I told you what would happen. Judy's in bed with Lester. . . . I saw her go in there and she's been in there for hours.'

'Is that all?'

'Shhh! I knew it would be Lester,' she said. 'All those fat, common men from Pennsylvania have sex in their boot-laces. But she must be absolutely stupid. Stupid, Kit.'

I wondered for a moment if Aimee had something of her own in mind as she leaned against me – young and safe and sure and unafraid. But I didn't think too long about it because she dug her knee into my ribs and said: 'I told you, didn't I? But I wish to God it had been Pip. I can't stand the idea of someone like Terrada in the family. It's like walking through the house with muddy boots on.'

I turned over and went back to sleep as she tucked me up and sighed over me in childish raptures and went back to bed.

CHAPTER

4

I had to pretend that I knew nothing, which was difficult at first because Terrada blossomed with a sort of embarrassed shyness, as if we had all caught him looking at himself in the mirror. He was restless, and he spent a lot of time looking out of the office window at the Monday morning sky. Then Judy appeared at our doorway and said, 'Which one of you guys is writing the *Ark Royal* story?'

'Me,' I said.

The British aircraft-carrier *Ark Royal* had been torpedoed and sunk by a German U-boat in the Mediterranean, and Wertenbaker had told me to give the story as much sympathy as I liked.

'It's on my list,' Judy said, 'so if you want any more material from London or Washington you'd better let me know quick.'

'I don't want anything from that Washington naval expert,' I told her. 'So you can skip that bit.'

'Are you going to be your own naval expert?' Judy said. She had the right to be sarcastic – to a point anyway.

'Yes, dammit,' I said to tell her that she had gone far enough.

Pip laughed and Judy said rather huffily that she'd give me everything that came in and I could do what I pleased with it.

I was being bold with Judy because I knew her secret. I felt superior because nothing gives a man an edge on a woman as much as the knowledge of some hidden if modest passion.

'What have you got, Lester?' she asked him very impersonally.

'The Russians are retreating around Moscow,' Terrada
said. He was blushing, in fact he was so helpless in his
embarrassment that I felt sorry for him. He didn't know
where to look or what to do with his hands. He kept
clearing his throat as if that was the only way to cope with
it.

'You ought to get something for that cough,' Judy said to
him. 'You obviously caught cold.'

'I'm all right,' he said.

'You'll only bring your germs in here if you don't do
something about it.'

'I haven't got a cold,' he said, and I noticed that he was
sweating profusely through the large pores of his cheek-
bones so that his eyes looked wet and cold.

'You look awful,' Judy said.

He looked awful because Judy seemed to be stripping
him of one of his natural rights – his sexual pride. I wondered why she did it, and when she turned her attention on
Pip she confused me a little more.

'Are you writing the Chungking story, or is Teddy
White?' she asked Pip, and this time she was a schoolmis-
tress asking her favourite pupil to recite his lesson.

'Teddy is. I'm doing the one on the Japanese mission to
Berlin.'

'That's Carol's,' Judy said. There were a dozen other
researchers we worked with – Carols and Ingrids and Joans
and Judiths and Esthers and Hildegardes. 'But I can take it
over if you like,' Judy said to him.

'That'd be nice,' Pip said. 'You'll write most of the story
anyway.'

Pip was a poor writer in the *Time* style. Strictly speaking
he wasn't interested in writing at all because his real passion
(as Wert had said) was situation not communication.

'Okay,' she said. 'I'll tell Carol and you can take me to
lunch.'

I wasn't at that lunch and what I know of it came from Pip

36

himself when he was looking back with a certain bitterness on those fate-ridden months of 1941. Lester was left in the office and I took a sandwich at Schrafft's on 42nd Street with Teddy White and Sam Salt who were still educating me. 'Old Schrafft,' Sam told me, 'is the inventor of the American stomach.' While I ate something wrapped in thick toast and mustard with pickles and coffee, Judy took Pip to an Italian restaurant over on Seventh Avenue, and when he told me about that lunch Pip said it was the first time he had noticed how tangible Judy's face was when you took a good look at it.

'I always found it tangible enough,' I told him. 'A private little face, a very stubborn, neat little face.'

'Okay. Okay. But there was always something you couldn't come to grips with when you saw Judy in and out of the office, or among other people. For two hours I sat two feet away from her in one of those booths you used to get in New York restaurants and I got a good look at her; and by the end of that meal I was bowled over.'

'By what?' I asked him.

'God knows.' Pip said. 'Character, I think. She had her own style, Kit. She always reminded me of a dog that kept burying things. But I think I must have dismantled her face that day and rebuilt it, and I was amazed to find how attractive it was. Alive, too. Even lovely when you looked close enough at each piece of it. It was only the whole that could look peaked. Maybe if I looked even closer that day I might have seen the iron under the skin, but I didn't see it until a couple of years later when I couldn't do anything about it.'

Judy told him over that lunch that she was very worried about him. 'You're spoiling your reputation when you argue so fiercely with Luce about the importance of the communists among the Chinese peasantry. You sound prejudiced, Pip. You're losing your objectivity.'

That was something else I had not attended – that particular editorial conference with Henry Luce. Judy had been in attendance as one of the senior researchers, and Pip and

Luce had quarrelled not so much about the communists in China, but about the effectiveness of Chiang Kai-shek as the man who would eventually rescue China. (This was three weeks before Peal Harbor.) Pip argued that Chiang Kai-shek had no roots in anything but the army, the big banking families, the corrupt middle classes and whatever foreign help he could get to do his fighting for him.

'That's the scenario,' Pip said, 'and that's the way we ought to look at it.' That was the way Pip himself would have to look at it when that conversation eventually came up before the House committee.

Luce argued that the Generalissimo was above party and beyond corruption, and that was the way we (U.S., *Time* and *Life*) were going to deal with him. There was no question of doubting his motives. 'And if it is that bad,' Luce said, 'maybe we can set him right.'

'With what?' Pip wanted to know.

But Pip had lost the day and Judy was trying to tell him so over lunch. 'You're upsetting Mr Luce,' she warned.

'Oh, for Christ's sake,' Pip said. 'Harry understands. It's nothing more than an old argument between us, only it's getting more primitive every time it comes up, which is why it's beginning to annoy me.'

'Then why argue at all?' Judy said.

'Because he's wrong and I'm right.'

'Well that doesn't do any good, so I'm going to shut you up next time.'

Pip laughed. 'You don't say . . .'

'I do say.'

'Are you aiming to save me from myself?' he asked teasingly.

'I might make it my life's work,' she said, and as they walked back to 49th Street along the avenues of cardboard waste and empty taxis she began to take up her responsibilities. 'What you need is someone to keep telling you that what you think and what you say is eventually what you are accused of in this world.'

'Why should that worry me?' he said.

'Not everybody understands your motives, Pip, and you ought to keep that in mind every time you open your mouth, because some day somebody will use everything you say against you.'

'Oh, bullshit,' Pip said – a rare departure for Pip when talking to a woman.

But he was flattered to feel that he had now been tucked under one of Judy's neat little wings. In fact there was sex under there too and I watched it working after lunch when Judy came around to our door to play another little elegy with him.

'Oh Pip . . .' she said softly as if she had some sudden need to tell him something personally and privately. She ignored Terrada.

'Yes, what is it, Judy?'

'Did you get that story on General Stilwell?'

'Yesterday. It's here somewhere.'

'Well I wouldn't trust the agency report on it, if I were you.'

'Okay.'

Later she made other excursions to give him advice and information, always ignoring Terrada, which meant that by now I was looking for signs of jealousy from Lester. Instead he seemed genuinely puzzled. He didn't show any hostility to Pip, or blame him in any way for Judy's behaviour. But now that sex was obviously on the way Lester was more and more out of his depth. In fact he seemed to expect to be robbed of his girl as if he had no right to expect anything else, and I think it was this curious futility that annoyed Judy and encouraged her to deliver more and more attention to Pip. In any case she stood in the doorway just before we all quit for the day and invited Pip out to Connecticut for the weekend.

Pip said 'Why not?', still inside the spell of that rediscovery of Judy's closely attractive face.

So Pip was alone with Judy that weekend – that is except for Aimee and the horses; and it was Aimee who told me what happened.

'American women,' Aimee said, 'I mean American women of that age, always try to turn men into naughty children. I couldn't stand it when Judy started mothering and bossing Pip and exposing herself at the same time. It was awful.'

'Now don't start exaggerating,' I told her as we ate our way down the menu of the Gloucester Inn, over on 51st Street.

'Honestly, Kit. I'm not exaggerating. They came up on Saturday, and Judy wouldn't let him go out. You know I almost had Pip on a horse, but she forbade it. Pip wanted to do it, I could tell, but she said she didn't want to have a broken neck on her conscience, and if he didn't want to make her sick with worry because of the weather (it was thawing like mad again) he wouldn't go anywhere near a horse, not even to pat its ears.'

'So he didn't?'

'Oh yes he did! That's the point. I told him I'd look after him and we'd stick to the gravel, so he got up on old Mintjulep – she's the one mare who can't put a foot wrong – he actually got up in the saddle and we were on the way out through the little cross-bar gate when Judy came running out and got hold of the bridle and said:

' "For God's sake get down, Pip. You look absolutely ridiculous on a horse. Ridiculous. . . ." '

Aimee laughed. 'In fact he did look rather silly. He was sitting there like Harpo Marx waiting to fall off. But I bet he would have stuck it out, only Judy wouldn't let go the bridle.'

'So?'

'So she went all feminine and motherly again. "Please, Pip, please," she kept saying. "Please get down." She was indecent, like her mother, and you know the way Judy's mother could get sometimes.'

'No I don't. But what did Pip say?' I asked.

'Nothing. He looked at me as if I ought to do the arguing for him. He's helpless sometimes, isn't he?'

'Sometimes.'

'I can't stand arguments with Judy because she doesn't really argue, she just makes you lose your temper and keeps needling you for ages afterwards. So all I could say to Pip was "Oh for God's sake, Pip, tell her to go to hell." '

'Excellent, tactful advice which he ignored.'

'Oh well, he knew anyway that if he didn't get off that horse Judy would have jumped into that damned Ford of hers and driven back to New York and left him there.'

'Never,' I said.

'How do you know?'

'Because I know Judy.'

'That's what you think,' Aimee said. 'She does it all with ultimatums. Mostly silent ones. You know how those women are. All they have to do is stamp their foot and say I'll never forgive you. How I hate women like that.'

I laughed but Aimee was upset. 'It's all very well for you to laugh,' she said, 'old Judy hasn't started working on you yet.' She pointed a fork at me. 'But wait till she does.'

'That'll be the day,' I said confidently.

'You don't think she'll try it on you? You don't think so?'

'No, I don't.'

'Will you bet?'

'I'm not a betting man, particularly on sex and women.'

'Anyway, she got him off Mintjulep and half an hour later they were having a terrible argument about Terrada. Then they made it up and drove off to the other side of Ridgeford for dinner. But you know what happened that night.'

'No, and for God's sake not so much serialisation. Just tell me.'

'Well I am telling you. Anyway I'm a night crawler,' she said over her blueberry pie. 'Ever since my first year at school when the seniors used to raid us in the middle of the night and jump on us with their knees I always wake up in the night and I have to walk around a bit to remind myself that I'm not going to get a knee in my stomach. That's how I woke up last time and saw Judy go into Lester. And it was exactly the same with Pip. Same bedroom, same bed. Can

41

you imagine it, Kit? She went over the whole scene again, exactly, but with a different man, in exactly the same place.'

'Now come on, Aimee, how do you know?'

'Because I heard them talking, and I heard Judy come out of the room just before morning. Exactly the same I tell you. Can you imagine it? Like animals.'

I didn't know what to say. After all I counted Judy and Pip and even Terrada as friends. I should defend them all, even to Aimee.

'Judy must have something in mind,' I said rather lamely.

'Yes – to get Pip. That's what she's got in mind.'

'You said you preferred Pip to Terrada. So what are you complaining about?'

'Pip's too good for her, and anyway it shouldn't happen that way, Kit!' Aimee looked hot and upset with indignation. 'People shouldn't have sex until they're married, and they shouldn't do it when there are other people in the same house.'

'Well I'm damned!' I said. 'You're a reactionary.'

'You're not going to tell me that Judy's right,' she said.

'I never judge,' I said.

'I know you don't. You just sit and watch, don't you? You look at absolutely everybody as if they're nothing to do with you.'

I blushed. If she pursued statements like that a little further she could be penetrating my carefully guarded secret of survival.

'Anyway,' I said. 'Being a horsewoman, I thought you'd have more natural theories about sex.'

'I have. For horses! And even sex between horses looks horrible. It puts you off.'

I laughed again.

'Laugh if you like, Kit,' she said, her mouth full, her eating delicious, 'but look what happens to a colt. You know that a colt is the only really complete horse, which is why colts are always so beautiful. Even more than fillies. Then what happens. They spoil it all. They always look ridiculous when they're coupling with a mare, and men do too.'

I was incredulous. 'How on earth do you know that?'

'Isn't that why sex is always done in the dark?' she said.

She had now been through a four-course meal of crab, lobster, salads, ice cream and blueberry pie. She had arrived at dark chocolates and coffee and I was watching her. Aimee wasn't a pretty girl but she was about to become a beauty, and she was just beginning to dress ahead of her age, so she looked gauche and badly finished. Her lipstick was hopeless, her rather gingery hair was drawn back tight and tied with a neat blue ribbon, and I sat there wondering at what moment now she would look at herself and see what was really there. She had squirted herself twice during the meal with a little spray of Chanel, and maybe that Chanel was the first of many unwitting corruptions of the spirit that would eventually bring Aimee to her tragic end.

But at the time she was still half-flower and half-filly and I was about to pay the bill and get back to our little mountain on 49th Street when she leaned over and said, 'You know what Pip did the next day – the Sunday morning?'

'He apologised for his bad behaviour?' I suggested.

'No, I'm serious,' she said. 'He heard me taking out Clockwork (the colt) and he rushed out and said "Wait for me and I'll come with you." '

'So you finally got him on a horse,' I said, anxious to finish with this and get back.

'No. I told him I didn't want him to come with me. Ever! Then I told him about Lester and Judy in the same bed as him and Judy.'

'By God you didn't!'

'I did. It serves Judy right, and Pip too.'

I was sitting up with money in my hand and I dropped it on the floor. 'What did Pip do to you?' I asked her as I groped around under the table. 'Knock you down?'

'He just said in that uppity way he has sometimes: "You shouldn't have told me, Aimee." So I said, "Why not?" And he said, "Because it's damned rude to begin with, and in any case why couldn't you leave it to Judy to tell me herself?" So I said, "You must be crazy. She'd never tell

43

you." Then he said,"Maybe not, but the choice was hers not yours." So I rode off in a terrible huff.'

'My God,' I said. 'I hope he doesn't tell Judy.'

'Why should he tell her?'

'He just might.'

'So why should I worry?'

'Because she'll chop you up into little pieces and then spend years and years grinding what's left of you into dust.'

'You don't like her do you?'

'Of course I do. But I know what Judy's like.'

'Pip won't tell her.'

'How do you know?'

'He told me so. You know what he did when I came back?'

I had learned by now to wait through Aimee's style, so I sat back to hear it out.

'He sat in the kitchen with me and told me the story of his life over breakfast. I always thought it was his father who was the missionary, which always seemed odd for a Lovell, but he said it was his mother who was the religious one. His father put his feet up all over China, while his mother made Christians out of idol-worshippers. He said his mother despised the Chinese and spent all her time trying to persuade them to stop being Chinese, whereas his father loved them all and never tried to teach them anything. In fact he told Pip to learn from them, particularly the way they believed in respect as a divine force – a much better system, he said, than Christian obeisance. Imagine! His mother made him learn Chinese. In fact he and his father spoke it like natives whereas his mother spoke it like a typewriter.'

'That sounds rather hard on the mother,' I said.

'That's what I told him. But he said No, she was a marvellous woman in everything except being a missionary, and the day she left China and went back to being an American she was a very tender woman, whereas his father just pined away up there in Brookline, Mass., and went back to China alone two years ago and put his feet up again,

44

in his old white linen suit, and died. And what do you think he died of?'

'Leprosy. Something frightful. A broken heart.'

'No. Chickenpox.'

'How?'

'Neglect. He got poisoned. It was all over before they knew it, and Pip said they brought his body back on the *Mariposa*, via Hawaii, and then cremated him in Boston and scattered his ashes up and down the Charles River behind a Harvard eight.'

'I don't believe a word of it.'

'I do. And it's just what Pip would do.'

As we cut back through Rockefeller Center, around the ice-rink, I said to Aimee: 'You know what's fascinating about that story, Aimee?'

'Yes. But tell me anyway.'

'That Pip told it to you at all. He would never have told that to Judy, in fact I doubt if he'd tell it to anyone else, so you ought to feel pretty damn flattered.'

'I just sat and listened,' she said and took my arm. 'Why do you think he chose to tell me?'

'Who knows?' I said.

But I knew. Pip saw what I saw. He was talking around the sweat-soaked boots to the American girl who didn't know how sensitive and conventional and safe and honest she really was. When we were about to part company at the glass doors of the Time-Life Building she squeezed my arm and said appealingly to me: 'You wouldn't like me like that, would you Kit?'

'What do you mean?'

'I mean . . . you wouldn't . . . would you?'

I should have pushed back a curl or stroked her rather firm little face or said something affectionate and flattering, but I couldn't do it to Aimee. I couldn't laugh either.

'No, Aimee, I wouldn't,' I told her.

'I thought so,' she said and sighed. Then she laughed. 'Anyway we'd look awfully silly, wouldn't we?' She left

45

me with a pathetic little wave, silk stockings crimpling and a backside which was still too large.

I watched her out of sight and I have often wondered since if Aimee might not be alive now if I had said 'yes' and carefully plucked the flower in the gentlest possible way so that she might have felt pleasure and beauty in sex rather than the pain and the violence that eventually made her life miserable and ended it sadly.

5

Judy now chose me, though why she did it is still a puzzle. She probably had to make some matriarchal point, supremacy over the male, the right to choose anyone or all from the tribe. Whatever it was, she had to have all of us to have one of us. On the next Tuesday I felt a light touch on my shoulder and Judy was looking down at me with soft green eyes which I hadn't noticed before.

'Aimee wants you to ride with her Sunday,' she said. 'Do you want to come out Saturday afternoon?'

Until then I had felt superior to them all. I was the man with the little smile of amusement, distance, cynicism.

'Well?' Her hand was kneading my shoulder very gently.

'All right,' I said. I couldn't resist the temptation to find out what she would do, and how she would do it.

And it was pleasant to speculate on my likely behaviour, although I was still more fascinated with Pip and Terrada and their problems, because they were now coming into conflict on direct questions about the war. It wasn't Russia and China this time, but the United States itself and where its policies would take it.

It was late in November, three weeks before Pearl Harbor, when Roosevelt persuaded Congress to amend the Neutrality Act to allow U.S. merchant ships carrying supplies to Britain to be armed. Pip slapped the tear-off sheet from the AP wire service on my desk and said, 'It ain't much, Kit, but thank God it's a step in the right direction.'

Terrada lifted his head and growled: 'You're determined to get us into that goddam war, aren't you?'

'You bet,' Pip said off-handedly.

Terrada took it seriously. He told Pip that he (Pip) and Roosevelt were going against history. Presidential pressure on Congress to involve U.S. ships was in effect a denunciation of the original Neutrality Proclamation of 1793, and contrary to the traditional policy outlined in Washington's Farewell Address of 1796 in which he had stated clearly and unequivocally that Americans should keep out of other people's affairs, and that anybody who meddled abroad was a fool and a dupe.

'And you know damn well what'll happen when the President puts guns on our merchant ships,' Terrada said.

'You bet,' Pip said again.

'Some crazy U.S. marine is going to take a shot at a German sub,' Terrada said grimly, 'and we'll be stuck into the war next day – which is obviously what the President is aiming at.'

'Stuff and nonsense,' Pip said.

'I tell you it's a policy of intervention and a bad one,' Terrada insisted and they went on quarrelling with their usual erudition about American policies for or against intervention in other people's affairs, Terrada quoting every President since Washington and Jefferson with declarations of non-alignment to prove that isolation and neutrality were correct; and Pip demonstrating that every President since Washington and Jefferson had been involved in foreign alignments or wars of intervention, particularly Adams, Grant, Polk, Teddy Roosevelt and Woodrow Wilson.

It was a bitter argument, but half an hour later they were teasing me about the coming weekend with Aimee, and I had enough sense to let them tease me without making any response. In any case they soon tired of it and I was sitting loyally at my desk writing the story of Rommel's breakthrough at Tobruk when Pip beckoned me outside. We walked around to the Coca-Cola machine and Pip leaned against the wall and said, 'The damnedest thing happened last night, Kit, and you'll never guess what.'

'No, I don't suppose I will,' I said. I thought it was something to do with Judy.

'I had a late night visit from a couple of FBI men,' he said.

I laughed. 'What do they want you for, Pip? Swearing allegiance to the British?'

But Pip was serious. 'No. It wasn't me they were after. It was Lester. It was the damndest thing,' he said, 'and I haven't made up my mind yet what to think of it.'

'You mean they're on to Lester for something he did?'

'I don't know. But they're obviously checking up on him.'

'Well I'll be damned.'

Pip hit the Coca-Cola machine hard to force it to give up its gold. 'I hate secret policemen,' he said. 'Ours and everybody else's.'

'Don't we all,' I said. 'But what did they want to know?'

'Lester's attitude. Now what in the hell is an *attitude*?' Pip said. 'They wanted to know who his friends are and whether to my knowledge – that's what they said – he still has any personal contact with the Russians.'

'Russians?'

'Yes. They even reminded me that he'd spent almost two years there.'

'What about his book – his thundering, biblical denunciations of the great experiment?'

'They were pretty bright boys, Kit,' he said. 'They told me they were more interested in what a man did with himself rather than what he claimed to be or what he wrote. So who were his contacts, et cetera, et cetera.'

'I suppose you mentioned Sanford and Bannerman and that Connecticut crowd.'

'I told them to go to hell. I wasn't going to spy on Lester.'

I think Pip really wanted to leave it there but I persisted. 'You haven't finished,' I said. 'What else happened?'

'Well . . . they were nice young men with clean cuffs

49

and crew cuts and they kept their tempers and said it wasn't a matter of spying on Lester, but of national security.'

'My God, what have they got on him?'

'I told them Lester considered himself the most loyal American since George Washington, and that's all I was going to say about him and to hell with them.'

'Good for you.'

'Maybe good for me, but those guys just sat there and said that every American considered himself George Washington. So they persisted and then they asked me about you.'

'Me? What have I got to do with it?'

'They were working on Lester, not you. They wanted to know if you are a close friend, or did you influence him in any way. So I blew my top and said that Lester was not susceptible to your English trickery and persuasions. But I told them I was. I said I was willing right now to take the United States into the war on the side of the English, which ought to at least put me in perspective for them. So what were they going to do about it.'

'What made you say a crazy thing like that?' I said.

Pip shrugged. 'Ah well, it's all shit really.'

'No, it isn't. Go on! What happened?' I said as we walked along the passageway to avoid the attentions of curious girl researchers – the Trudys, Junes, Abigails and Muriels who wanted to join our gossip and play flirtatious little games with Pip.

'I decided to give them the kind of answer they wanted, although it was against my better judgment. I told them he hated the Russians, and in all our editorial conferences he was as good as Congressman Dies and no help to the Russians at all. I told them Lester was the kind of guy who would denounce his best friend if he thought he was betraying the republic. I gave them a lot of that Connecticut farmhouse gaff, and I said he was even suspicious of the British, and would never accept anything they said at face value. No, by God, not even from you. And then I told them that I had never met a man who limited himself so much to being an American.'

'Are you going to tell Lester about it?' I asked Pip quietly as we reached the door.

'Hell – no! It would only worry the poor guy to death,' Pip said, 'but I'd love to know what they're on to him for.'

We went into the office and Lester was standing at the window staring out over the city the way Washington must have looked out over the Delaware wondering if he'd ever make it. In fact destiny was always beckoning Lester, his big hands tangled in his pockets. I suppose that was why he kept himself a little reserved from the rest of us. It must have struck Pip that way because he suddenly threw the subject into the middle of the room as if he couldn't help himself.

'Kit and I were just wondering what you think of the FBI, Les?' he asked as we settled down to do some of *Time*'s work.

Terrada seemed to jump a little; he didn't like the question at all. 'Somebody has to do it,' he said, and in an instant his face was covered in sweat and I could see it coming through his shirt. He sat down and started to beat heavily on his typewriter and I exchanged a puzzled look with Pip.

Seeing the effect it was having on Terrada, Pip was glad to drop the subject, and I forgot all about it until 8.30 the next morning when I was telephoned from the desk downstairs in the Murray Hill and the clerk told me that two men were on the way up to see me. I was reading Dreiser's *Jennie Gerhardt* (which Wertenbaker had given me) over the remains of my breakfast, which was on one of those marvellous trolleys American hotels use, and I just had time to put the book face-down and take a last gulp of coffee when I heard the knock at the door.

Two young men. Clean cuffs and crew cuts. I didn't have to think twice.

'Mr Quayle?' one said, holding something in his hand.

'Yes.'

He flashed a card at me. I never did see it and he said:

'Sorry to interrupt your breakfast, although we calculated that you'd be through by now. Are you?'

'Exactly on time,' I said.

'Good. Can we come in?'

They were in already, and I walked ahead and made some ridiculous, housewifely gesture of pulling up the unmade bed.

'Don't worry,' the second man said, and though I ought to give some sort of character to them, what character did they have except that everything untrainable seemed to have been trained out of them.

One of them did all the talking, and when his companion called him 'Blue' I think it was a sudden failure in his discipline to reveal even that much. But Blue had a mass of freckles, which seemed significant. What I remember of the other one was his posture, leaning casually against the wall near the window, legs crossed and arms folded as if he had to keep the whole room in view in anticipation of an invasion through the door. It is funny now, but it wasn't so funny then.

'We know you're not an American citizen,' Blue told me, and he sat down at the little oak desk that the old Murray Hill had provided for me. 'You're in the United States for a short training period. Another six weeks, isn't it?'

'That's right.'

'Where will you go when you leave the United States?'

'I don't know,' I said stiffly to show them that it was none of their business. But in fact I felt guilty because I did have something to hide from these men.

I was in the United States at Henry Luce's invitation but I was also here because the British wanted me here. At my military age, with a war on, I couldn't go off casually to the United States simply because I wanted to, even as a war correspondent. I had to get permission, and when I had gone to the Deputy Director of Military Intelligence (responsible for war correspondents) and told him that I had been asked to go to New York for three months to learn how *Time* worked so that I could work for them somewhere in the war, the DDMI said he knew all about it. He had read the intercepted cables and he thought it a whacking good idea for me to go.

'Better someone on our side in a job like that, than someone from the other side.'

So I was here as a British desirable, and though nobody else knew about it, Blue and his friend would be justified if they wanted to grill me about any extra motive I might have for being in the United States. But I knew that was not why they were here, in fact Blue turned on a little game of one-upmanship.

'Will you go to Russia when you've finished here?' he said.

'I don't know,' I told him. 'You'd better ask Henry Luce.'

'It's not that important. Have you ever been to Russia, Mr Quayle?'

'No. Not yet.'

'Not yet? Why? Would you like to cover that war? I mean it's obviously a pretty good assignment from a professional point of view. Wouldn't you say?'

'Yes.'

'Yes to which question, Mr Quayle?'

'Any one you like,' I said.

'You seem a bit jumpy. What's the matter?'

'No. I'm quite happy,' I said nervously.

Blue laughed. 'We're not here to frighten you,' he said. 'Just to ask your help if you're willing to give it. And I'm sure you are.'

'Help about what?'

'Nothing much. We know you work with Phillip Lovell and Lester Terrada, and we wondered if you could tell us something about their friendship, that's all.'

'Tell you what about their friendship?'

'How close they are, for instance. Are they *very* good friends?'

I was still young enough and times then were still naive enough for their direction to escape me. So I missed the point.

'Of course they're good friends,' I said. 'They argue a lot, but it doesn't spoil their friendship.'

'But how close are they? Is it a normal sort of friendship? Would you say that it's normal, or is it abnormal in some way?'

I got the point then and I suppose I did the right thing. I laughed loudly. 'You're definitely barking up the wrong tree there,' I said, 'if that's what you're worried about.'

'We're not barking up any tree, Mr Quayle,' Blue said sternly. 'We're checking up on possibilities. Can you tell us anything about Lester Terrada's work?'

'I don't know anything about it,' I said, hostile again.

'But you work in the same room in the same department.'

'I never read what Lester writes.'

'Why not?'

'Because it depresses me. He makes me feel that we're losing the war.'

'But he's writing about the Russian front, not the British.'

'Same war,' I pointed out.

'Have you ever been to Russia, Mr Quayle?'

'You already asked me that.'

'Have any Russians or Russian sympathisers ever visited Lester Terrada in his office?'

'No. Can I ask you something?'

'Go ahead.'

'Why are you asking all these questions about Lester and the Russians?'

'That's our business.'

'In that case all I can say is that Lester is the most American American I've ever met. He even makes me feel ashamed for not wanting to become an American. And that's about all I can tell you about him, no matter how many questions you ask. So do you mind if we cut this short because I have to get to work.'

'You don't punch a clock.'

'No. But I've got a lot to do.'

'Okay.' Blue got up from the desk. 'You've been very helpful and we appreciate it. You want a lift to your office?'

I thought Yes, then I thought No.

Blue laughed. 'I leave it to you. But one thing more.' He walked over to the breakfast trolley and picked up *Jennie Gerhardt*. 'I see you're reading the American writer, Theodore Dreiser.'

'Yes.'

'You like him?'

'Nobody to touch him,' I said.

'Did you know he was a communist?'

'Was he?'

'A member of the American communist party,' Blue told me.

'You don't think I should read him?' I asked. I was playing the game as before, but it was also a genuine question.

'I'm not saying that,' Blue answered quickly. 'It's all part of your job, I suppose.'

His companion moved out front – a look-out for possible attack coming from any one of the brown doors along the old corridor. Blue put on his hat with three fingers (I forgot to mention the hats) and said, 'Goodbye Mr Quayle. Thanks for your help.'

I closed the door before he asked me again if I wanted a lift. I didn't want a lift because I knew that if I sat in a car with these two men I would be cowering handcuffed in a corner while they drove me to Grand Central to put me on a train back to Chicago. And though it was no more than a weird little farce for me, I wondered what it might be like if they were really after you. Or what it was like for Terrada, who had shadows and mistakes and political dynamite in his background. Even his re-apostasy was under suspicion, and I felt sorry for Lester. Like Pip I wondered what Blue and his friend were really after.

We worked some Saturday mornings so the office was still fairly full and I felt very conspicuous as I carried my overnight bag and walked with Judy holding my arm along the corridors to the lift. Judy knew almost everybody on both *Time* and *Life* floors so she got the looks, I didn't. But I think she was teasing me because she seemed to be enjoying it.

Judy had parked her Ford in one of the cement caverns of someone's apartment block on Park Avenue and we walked across town without saying a word. When we reached the Ford she asked me if I wanted to drive. I shook my head and we set off in silence. Halfway out along Park Avenue she swore at the heater which was working badly, but once we were on the Freeway she simply opened up the Ford and we were suddenly driving somewhere to do something. In fact there was a curious, sexual insinuation in our long and purposeful silence. I think Judy knew it and may have planned it that way. But I still didn't quite know what she expected of me. She mixed a very strong cocktail the moment we got to the farmhouse and said, 'You never get drunk, do you?'

'Not so far,' I said.

That was not strictly true because in the retreat from Salonika I had poured a half bottle of gin down my very dry throat thinking it was water that happened to taste of petrol. I had never tasted gin before and the result was a day and a half of blind drunkenness – chased by five German tanks across the plains of Marathon. But I counted that an accident.

'Well, I don't like drunkenness but I'd love to get you drunk,' Judy said, 'just to see what's underneath that untouchable English pose of yours.'

'You wouldn't find anything,' I told her. 'I hide nothing.'

'You hide everything. Which is what makes me awfully suspicious.'

'Suspicious of what?' I said nervously. Those FBI men had given me a sudden complex about my presence in the United States.

'You're afraid of sex, aren't you?' she said.

I laughed. 'I'm afraid of you,' I told her.

'Oh, I know that,' she said off-handedly as if it was

56

hardly worth disputing; although I wasn't afraid of her at all then. 'But you don't ever want to talk about sex, do you?' she said.

'Not if I can help it.'

'Well,' she said, her eyebrows clamped together, 'I just want you to know that I think sex has two objectives. One is to bring honest lovers together, and the other one is to keep them together if it works. But I don't suppose you would agree with that, would you?'

'Wholeheartedly,' I said.

Judy was rattling the swizzle stick in her drink and standing over me aggressively as if there was a bit of a threat in everything she was saying. 'You really aren't like an American, are you?' she said. 'You couldn't be mistaken for one.'

She was rocking on her heels, challenging me to stand up and face her and become her sexual equal. But I knew that any sexual approach to Judy now would reduce me to a non-equal, and I decided that this must be the way the American matriarchal system worked. I longed then for Aimee to appear and get me out of this mess.

'I'm going to get you drunk,' Judy said, 'for your own good. So finish that martini for heaven's sake.'

'I'll drink two cocktails and that's all,' I told her. 'I don't want a hangover when I'm chasing Aimee over those fences and hedges tomorrow.'

'Oh, Aimee's a child,' Judy said contemptuously. 'And that's another reason why I'm very suspicious of you. You're afraid of adult women, aren't you?'

At this point I think I knew what had happened to Pip and Terrada. They had both fallen for this diminishment, this challenge to their masculinity, although Judy had probably used a different method in their case.

'I'm not afraid of adult women,' I said to her, raising my glass to her. 'I told you, Judy, I'm afraid of you.'

'We'll see about that later,' she said.

But Judy considered the rest of the afternoon a failure because I didn't seem able to fit myself into any of her shapes and plans. She stacked four records of a Brahms concerto on the automatic record changer and every time a record fell it sounded like a musical pistol shot. I couldn't stand it. I got up and walked out, crushing up and down the gravel roadway. It was cold without a coat but listening to classical music was one thing I couldn't do in New York. I could go to a theatre, a cinema, eat in expensive restaurants, even swim on one cold day off Littlehampton, but the only time I felt that I was deserting my country in time of war was when I sat in someone's house listening quietly to serious music.

But I didn't want to explain that to Judy, and I hadn't gone far up the road when a Plymouth station-wagon skidded to a stop on the gravel and Aimee got out of it. She said goodbye to the driver who sped off, and Aimee waited for me to catch up with her.

'You were looking so miserable,' she said, 'that I told Pete to let me off. Were you thinking of the war or something?'

'I suppose I was,' I said, and Aimee took my arm and hopped and skipped a little to encourage me.

'Well, I'll soon knock that out of you,' she said. 'I've been waiting for you all week, and if you come into the barn I'll show you what I've been dying to do.'

The barn was the stables, and I followed her in. She turned the light on, the horses snuffed and pawed in response to our presence. Aimee went straight to Mintjulep's stall and took down a set of boxing gloves that were hanging on the bridle hook.

'Do you know how to box?' she asked me.

'Certainly.'

'Then put these gloves on and let's have a fight.'

Aimee was the fighting kind. It was her age and her body.

'You and me?' I said. 'I can just see it.'

But she was serious and she threw the pair of gloves at me.

'Oh no,' I said. 'I'm not putting on the gloves with you. Not a chance. Not even for a joke.'

'Why not?'

'Not in a million years,' I told her. 'So forget it.'

'But I want to learn how to fight,' she said. 'I need to, Kit. I have to. And it won't hurt you.'

'It won't hurt me but it might hurt you,' I pointed out. 'Anyway what do you want to know how to fight for?'

'I want to knock somebody down.'

'Oh no. Not me, Aimee.'

'No. Not you, silly. There are two people I want to hit hard and I want to do it properly.'

'Who are they?'

'Never mind who they are.'

'No!' I said.

'All right. If you won't box with me, then at least teach me how to do it, Kit. Go on. Put the gloves on and just show me. I borrowed them specially.'

Aimee was very persuasive and it seemed harmless enough so I said, 'All right. If Mrs Jack London could do it, why not you?' I helped Aimee on with the gloves and then tied one of my own and tightened the other with my teeth.

'Do you really know about boxing, Kit?' she said again as we stood there with our fists weighted like loaves of bread.

'I was a schoolboy champ,' I said. 'But before we start I still have to know who you intend to knock down. A man or a woman?'

'A man, of course. Two of them. And they're both asking for it.'

'Who are they?'

'It's personal, Kit, so don't ask me too much about them. It's got something to do with my female dignity.'

'All right,' I said, and I told her that there was one primitive rule about fighting. 'You hold your left straight out to ward off your opponent, to keep him so far away he can't hit you. Then, when you see the chance, you simply hit him hard with your right. All boxing is based on a variation of that principle.'

I had demonstrated with my left and right what I meant,

though I didn't deliver any blow or touch her. But Aimee said: 'Well, go on! Do it.'

'Oh no. I'm not going to touch you. But you can try it out on me if you like. Stand sideways a little, keep your left out so I can't reach you, then swing forward and hit me with your right.'

Aimee was very quick. She hit me hard with her right before I knew it and I staggered back.

'My God,' I said. 'You really mean it, don't you.'

'But it's marvellous, Kit. Let's do it again.'

This time I blocked her right and reversed the situation so that she suddenly found my right in her face, though again I didn't touch her.

'Fabulous!' Aimee shouted. 'Show me how to do that.'

My methods were a primitive nineteenth-century style and my expertise was limited, but it was easy to teach Aimee the simple one-two. Twice after that she hit me hard with her right and I taught her how to tuck her elbows in defensively, and how to roll with a blow rather than stand up to it. We were standing in the dirt passageway of the stable like schoolboys learning the rudiments in the school gym and she didn't want to stop. In fact she was a natural, and when I finally told her I'd had enough I was out of breath, my cheeks were grazed and I had bitten my tongue. In fact my stomach was sore from a couple of very low jabs. But I still hadn't touched her.

'Just once more. Please, Kit,' she said.

So I shaped up one last time, and Aimee came at me one-two, one-two. I held up my arms, backed away, and stepped on Judy.

'What in heaven's name are you up to?' Judy said.

'Oh, go away, Judy,' Aimee shouted. 'You'll spoil everything.'

Judy took it all in and said, 'My God, I'm speechless. I've never seen anything like it in my life. It's disgusting.'

'Oh, shut up, Judy,' Aimee said calmly.

Judy turned on me then. 'Don't you realise that if you hit a woman on the breast you can give her cancer?'

'I'm not hitting her,' I pointed out. 'She's hitting me.'

'What for?'

'None of your business,' Aimee said. 'It's between Kit and me.'

'That's obvious,' Judy said, and I couldn't help feeling that she was handling me very well. I felt a fool. But then she spoiled it. 'If this is what you prefer to Brahms . . .' she said to me.

That was too obvious so I regained some composure. I told her it must be the cocktails she had given me.

'You mean two martinis,' Judy said contemptuously as she walked out.

Aimee laughed happily and hit me with her right when I wasn't expecting it. 'You beat her,' she said. 'You floored her.'

'No, I didn't,' I said. 'And she's right, Aimee. You may get hit in the wrong place so for God's sake don't ever shape up to a man. Even as a joke.'

'I'm not going to joke.'

'In that case you'd better hit whoever it is with a rolling pin.'

'Oh no! I want to do it like a man, face to face. One-two, just like you showed me.'

'In that case I insist you tell me who it is. That's fair, Aimee. So out with it.'

'One is a boy named Jack who is always mauling me when I'm not looking. He tries to touch me everywhere and it's horrible and he thinks I'm in love with him. The other one is Lester Terrada.'

'Lester!'

'Yes. I can't stand him. I can't stand the way he makes everybody feel they shouldn't hurt him. How does he do it? And you know what, Kit?'

'No, what?'

'He doesn't behave like an American. You're much more like an American than he is.'

I told her not to say such things about Lester, and I pointed out what Judy had said – that I could never be mistaken for an American.

61

'See!' she said. 'Even you are trying to protect him. How does he do it? Just how does he make everybody feel sorry for him, that's what I'd like to know. It's disgusting.'

I thought about it and decided that Aimee was certainly right. Lester always seemed to inspire the mother in a man. 'But what do you want to hit him for? You haven't explained.'

'I don't have to explain. I just want to show him that he's taken in everybody else but not me,' she said. 'He's got you all bamboozled and I hate that. I don't want him in my family, even ten times removed. I really do hate him, Kit.'

'You're crazy,' I said but I couldn't help laughing and I left her to the horses and the mash and the manure-collecting, and the game she played with a whip when the field mice who lived in the rafters scurried down the side walls without fear or fright to confront her across the floor of the stable. Aimee never managed to hit them with the whip and they always came back as if they knew she wasn't really trying.

As for me, I went back to Judy who was preparing a neat dinner in the kitchen and I told her I had decided to go back to England next week if I could get a seat on a clipper.

'But your time isn't up,' she said. 'You've got at least another month.'

'I know, but I've got to go.'

'Why? What suddenly changed your mind?'

'I don't know. Brahms, I think.'

'Who?'

'It doesn't matter.'

'Well I don't think Henry Luce is going to like it.'

'He'll understand,' I said. 'Wert'll explain it to him.'

'In that case I haven't much time, have I?' she said with an amused look which surprised me. She had obviously decided to be charming, and she came across the kitchen towards me as if she was going to make up for lost time. At that moment I saw what Pip saw – the soft green eyes, the perfect nose and delicate mouth. The whole pyramid of her face became gentle and attractive when you saw it like that.

We exchanged no more than a light kiss, but I swear it was a promise of more to come if I wanted it.

It was spoiled by Aimee, who came into the kitchen to get a Coca-Cola from the icebox, and Judy told her to clean the grit from her fingernails and to get out of her pants and into a proper dress if she wanted to dine with us.

'You stink of horse,' Judy said.

'Better a horse stink than Lester Terrada's,' Aimee replied.

Judy turned around and slapped her hard.

Aimee stood like a rock for a moment. She was breathless and I thought she was going to hit back. But big yellow tears began rolling down her red cheeks. 'Hit me as much as you like,' she burst out, 'but I'm going to hit him one day.' And she made a vicious pass with her fists in the air under Judy's nose.

'If you ever dare touch him,' Judy cried, 'I'll make absolutely certain that all those horses are sold and that you're packed off to Aunt Ephie in Maine.'

'You can't touch those horses. They're mine.'

'They're nobody's. They belong to the trust, like everything else around here, and you know it.'

'They're more mine than yours.'

'Tell that to the trustees next time you see them. If I say they ought to go, they'll go. So watch your step.'

'I'm going to hit him,' Aimee sobbed, 'and if you do anything about those horses, Judy I'll . . . I'll do something awful. I'll think of something terrible.'

Judy was calm and at ease in the quarrel, Aimee was resentful and broken. Her muddy tears were more like sweat, they seemed to pour out of her red cheeks rather than her eyes and they were all over the place. She grimaced angrily and accusingly at me and left.

'She's ridiculous,' Judy said, 'and so are you for encouraging her.'

'She won't do anything,' I said.

'Oh, yes she will,' Judy insisted. 'And so will I. She's going to end up a lesbian if she isn't careful.'

'I'll never believe that,' I said.

In fact that remark made me so angry that I wanted to tell her that Aimee was far more feminine and far more attractive than Judy herself. There were many other things I wanted to tell Judy; but I never did because personal comment meant personal replies, and I guarded my life against that sort of involvement.

'She doesn't want you to marry Lester,' I said to Judy. 'That's what she's mad about.'

Judy laughed and poured me out a cocktail from a glass jug she kept in the ice box. 'Why should I marry someone like Lester?' she said. 'If I had to pick anyone from the 29th floor I'd pick Wert, or Pip, or even you. Lester needs a mother and a flag-bearer, and though I can be one or the other I can't be both.'

'Why are the FBI so interested in him?' I asked her.

'So they got to you too,' she said.

'Yes.'

'Lester's taking a job in Washington so they're going through the usual check-up.'

'Is that all?'

'Why? What did you think?'

'I don't know. But he didn't tell Pip about it.'

Judy looked very pleased to hear that. 'Didn't he?' she said.

'No.'

'It's that odd relationship of theirs,' she said. 'They get very tricky with each other when they get involved in real things. They're like two friends competing for the same woman.'

'You, Judy?'

'Don't be silly. It's this thing they're involved with about America. They can't leave it alone, and they can't separate themselves from it. That's why I've been telling Lester that he ought to go to Washington.'

'What for?'

'Because he's too much in awe of Pip and all Pip stands for. Lester needs to get away from him.'

'Did Lester tell you that?'

Judy was putting plates in the oven to heat and she took off her perfect little oilcloth apron. 'He didn't have to tell me. Do you know what their real trouble is, Kit?'

She was easing me out of the kitchen into the living-room.

'Is there any real trouble between them?' I said.

'You know what I mean. They've got nothing in common except the wrong thing.'

I waited for more, but Judy said she had finished being perceptive and told me to go and get washed.

Later when I sat down to dinner Aimee walked in demurely wearing a tight, ice-blue dress which showed all her puppy fat and filled out her charming, youthful slump. I supposed that she and Judy were used to quarrelling and smacks, but I knew that Aimee was being careful now because she was afraid of losing her horses. She was also worried about me, and when Judy left us after dinner for a few moments Aimee whispered:

'I'm going to sit here all night if necessary.'

'What for?'

'I don't want you to go to bed with her,' Aimee said.

'I don't intend to go to bed with her,' I said.

'But she intends it. I'm going to walk into your bedroom every half hour to make sure.'

'You don't have to go that far,' I told her. 'My honour and my sex are quite safe, I swear it.'

'No, they aren't. Not with her. And if you do give in I'll never speak to you again.'

Judy returned and knew that we were whispering about her, so she told Aimee the horses were restless and to go and see about them.

'You left a light on in the barn,' Judy said.

'I didn't.'

'Yes you did. Go and see.'

Aimee left us, to check, and Judy sat near me and ruffled my hair and stroked my neck with gentle fingertips.

'Well?' she said.

'I'm a married man,' I told her.

'I didn't know that,' she said.

'I suppose I should have told you.'

'Why? Anyway, where's your wife?'

'Cairo. She's a nurse in one of our military hospitals.'

'What's she like?'

Judy was still stroking my neck. 'She's a Catholic,' I said, 'and very moral.'

'What about you?'

The hand was still on my neck.

'I'm not a Catholic, and I'm not very moral,' I told her, and she laughed. 'But I'm loyal,' I said, 'and I suppose that makes a difference.'

Judy dropped her hand. 'How. funny,' she said and laughed again. 'How very funny.'

But I'm not sure that she thought it funny at all. I don't think Judy ever forgave me for letting it go so far, and she didn't come into my room that night and I didn't go into hers. Aimee came into my bedroom twice, jumped on my bed, hit me once on both knees with an expert schoolgirl torture, pulled my bedclothes off the second time and finally left, satisfied but furious because she was sure now that Judy was going to choose Terrada.

'Pip's too weak for her,' she said. 'She really wants that steel puddler, doesn't she?'

CHAPTER

6

A few days before I was due to sail with a convoy leaving Delaware Bay for Liverpool, the Japanese bombed Pearl Harbor, and America became a different place and Pip and Terrada became different men. Or rather they were still the same men but circumstances put them into a new situation.

It surprised me at the time that Americans were not instantly aware that they were now totally and irrevocably at war, and that everything about their lives would change. The quiet Sunday morning routine on the 29th floor was the same as every other working Sunday. The deserted New York streets below were the same, so was the air and the atmosphere and the everyday suburban anticipation of lunch, dinner, cocktails, and the Monday morning routine to follow. I had never realised before how little Americans knew or felt about war (why should they). I had been in London when we were declared at war, and an hour after Chamberlain's speech telling us about it you could feel the city sucking in its breath. I was in Paris the next day and it was already a war city, even if it was a phoney-war city.

This isn't a personal recollection of the war but the story of what happened to Pip and Terrada, so the real point of interest is what began to change them on that Sunday morning. Perhaps Pip was the only one who knew what to expect. His curious feeling for knowing 'what is' opened up a mighty vista of the years to come: huge sea and air battles across the Pacific Ocean, American armies marching across Europe to meet the Russians in Berlin, the war ended by some extraordinary new weapons. No one else saw it so exactly, and I only appreciated it later because at the time Pip's speculations were no more than fantasies to me. War so far had been too dangerously uncertain to see it going clearly in any direction.

The strange thing about it was Pip's interest in Europe and Terrada's interest in Japan. It should have been the other way round. But Pip was always a global man whereas Terrada was pure and simple American, and now that Japan had tried to rape the Republic it was Japan who had to be pursued and destroyed. Germany and Italy were ignored because they had not yet declared war on the United States so they didn't stir Lester's temper.

'But it's all the same damned war,' Pip pointed out.

'I don't care whether it's the same war or not,' Terrada argued. 'The whole continent of Europe can die of military exhaustion as far as I'm concerned. It's Japan we have to deal with. Japan is young and brutal and wants to try itself out on us. So she'll blast us clean out of the Pacific if she can, and even get a grip on the West Coast if we don't hit back quick and hard.'

'You're a proper little-American at heart, Les,' Pip said, 'which makes you a better American than I am, I suppose.'

Terrada didn't deny it. He blew out his cheeks and said in an embarrassed way: 'I'm quitting *Time* and moving to Washington next week, Pip. I thought you ought to know.'

'Well, I'll be damned,' Pip said. He said he was delighted and I think he was finally relieved of that worrying brush with the FBI. 'So that's why they were checking up on you.'

Terrada nodded. He looked the way I had felt as a twelve-year-old boy when I told my parents that I had just won the school's high-diving contest – proud, modest, vain and damned superior. I couldn't help liking Terrada at that moment.

The real quarrel between them came later, after an editorial meeting on the Monday which I did not attend. They both came into the office in a curiously silent mood as if they had just been arguing bitterly and were trying, by silence, to separate themselves. By now Germany and Italy had declared war on the United States, a move that has always been difficult to understand because even Roosevelt would have found it difficult automatically to declare war in Europe. So Pip and Terrada were now in dispute about real allies and real enemies. America was technically on the same side as the Russians, and that was a fact that had to be faced. Terrada insisted that it made no difference, and after another long silence between them Pip finally blurted out:

'You want to go on behaving towards the Russians as if they were a more serious enemy than Germany.'

'You're damn right,' Terrada said. 'I don't like the Nazis, Pip, but that's no reason why we have to become Russia's allies.'

'The Russians are probably going to win the war,' Pip said. 'So what'll you do then?'

Terrada laughed. 'I'll face that miracle of arms when it happens,' he said.

They went on arguing in the same vein, and inevitably it came around to China as well. Terrada didn't want the United States to give any help to the Chinese communist guerrillas in Yenan. 'Why should we help your friends the reds any more than we should help the Russians?' Terrada said. 'They'll only use it for their own ends.'

It was the first time I had heard him personalise their argument by calling the Chinese communists Pip's 'friends'. It was so unusual that Pip was stung. 'The Chinese in Yenan have been fighting the Japanese without let-up for ten years,' he said, 'while United States Marines have been beating up Chinese women in Shanghai brothels and aping the goddam English in their officers' clubs. What do you want us to do, Les? Fight a separate war?'

'We don't have to help communists, Pip,' Terrada said. 'I admit it's a long-term view but it's the right one for the United States.'

Pip got up. 'So it's going to be a neat little American war all by itself,' he said and walked out in disgust.

But they got over it and they were back to their old neutrality next day. They also organised a farewell party for me in Pip's flat and asked me who I wanted along. I wanted all the 29th floor because they were all my friends. The only outsider I asked Pip to include was Aimee.

'I'll be sorry to part with Aimee,' I told Pip. 'In six months, a year at the most, Aimee's going to blossom like a summer rose.'

'Without the horses.'

'My view exactly,' I said.

Pip became reflective and a little sad. 'Pity about Aimee,' he said. 'Do you really want her along?'

'She'll give Judy something to keep her eye on besides you and Lester,' I said.

'And Kit Quayle! Come on now, Kit, admit it.'

I knew what he meant and I thought I had better be indignant. 'I swear I never touched Judy,' I said.

'A likely story.'

'Ask Aimee. She made sure of it.'

Pip suddenly became serious. 'You mean it, Kit?'

'I swear it.'

'Amazing,' Pip said. 'I was sure Judy had planned your seduction.'

'I didn't know about it,' I lied. 'Furthermore, I ought to warn you that Aimee's going to knock down anybody who is fool enough to marry Judy,' I said. 'I trained her myself.'

I told Pip then about the boxing lessons and he thought it was marvellous. 'That explains a hell of a lot of English-women,' he said. 'You bring 'em all up as boxers.'

'Shush.'

'What did Judy say about it?'

'She threatened to cut Aimee off without a penny.'

'I'll bet she did. Only I wonder whose penny it really is,' Pip said.

I would learn later that Pip was right again. It was all Aimee's money, held in trust for her by an amalgam of lawyers and banks. Judy was no more than a secondary and minor beneficiary who nonetheless influenced the trustees because they considered her closest to Aimee and her best and most influential adviser.

'Okay. It's your party,' Pip said. 'So we'll invite little old Aimee, and all those miaowing kittens from the 29th floor can have a rapturous time teasing Judy when they hear that Aimee's a horse freak.'

He asked me then what Luce thought of my departure.

'He took it very well,' I said, 'but Wert paved the way for me.'

I had explained to Luce that I didn't think I was a *Time* sort of writer, and he had told me in his curiously embarrassed way not to worry.

'You've got your own future to think of, so it's your problem and your mistake,' he said. 'Pity for you it didn't work out.'

Our agreement had specified that either side could call it off. I offered to refund the bulk of my pay and return my airfare. Bur Luce wouldn't hear of it. He said they would pay me up to the end of our agreement and my fare back to London or to wherever I was going. It was generous and I felt guilty about the whole affair until I reported it to Pip.

'Oh shit on that,' Pip said. 'Harry's always a generous guy but you don't owe anybody anything. They've had their money's worth.'

Maybe. Maybe. In any case I was glad to be going back whence I had come. The war was my only home, and when I was out of it I was in a foreign country.

Pip's party was the usual 1941 New York party until Pip and Terrada quarrelled again. We sat around in couples and groups drinking whisky and bourbon and clear, cold martinis mixed by Judy. We listened to Hildegarde, and an unknown folk singer whom someone had discovered on uncommercial records – Burl Ives. We talked about the war, gracious living, dilettantism and the current New York literary game which was proving or disproving that Hemingway's description of sex in a sleeping bag was possible. *For Whom the Bell Tolls* was just out, and Robert Jordan and the Spanish girl, Maria, had made the earth move in a sleeping bag, which was an intellectual challenge on two levels to people like us. The only person who didn't think the technical arguments funny was the straitlaced Aimee who got a grip on my sleeve and said:

'It's all so crude and childish. Don't they ever talk about anything else?'

'Like what?' I said.

'Well . . . . I mean do they always kid around like this about sex? Don't they ever stop?'

'Yes. When they're working.'

'But it's absolutely boring,' she whispered fiercely and abandoned me.

She pulled on her rather ratty old beaver coat and left, and I felt sorry for her. Aimee was having a bad time fitting in anywhere except the stables. She couldn't understand her own troublesome, childish morality, which was too conventional and real to be believed, even by Aimee herself. Sex, vulgarity and love were separate items in Aimee's life, and how they would all hurt her!

With Aimee gone I felt a little lost. But then Pip and Terrada began to discuss Hemingway's interpretation of the Spanish War.

It was the first time I had heard about Terrada's once-active support for the Spanish Republic. Terrada criticised Hemingway's sentimentalising of the International Brigade, and Pip reminded him that in 1937 he, Terrada, had been one of the speakers at a rally in Philadelphia to raise money for the Brigade.

'Where did you get that piece of information from?' Terrada demanded, surprised that anyone, least of all Pip, would know about his activities as an obscure supporter of Republican Spain.

'A friend of yours, Jack Stoppard the bastard, was there and he told me the other day that he remembered you at that meeting sweating like hell and singing the Internationale at the top of your voice. It was you wasn't it, Lester?'

'Sure it was me. But I was very young in those days and I was taken in by all that intellectual hoo-ha you like so much.'

'It wasn't hoo-ha. Those guys were in it.'

'But you weren't, Pip,' Terrada said, 'so you can't stand there with a martini in your hand and justify it to me. You weren't involved.'

'I wasn't involved because I never get involved,' Pip said coldly.

Inevitably they swerved off into their usual dispute about American intervention or non-intervention. Terrada went on arguing that if the Spanish Republic had been strong enough and deeply enough implanted it wouldn't have needed any outside help, even from American volunteers, even against the German and Italian airforces and armies.

'Of all the damnedest theories,' Pip protested. 'How d'you think Washington won Yorktown, which gave us our deeply implanted republic? In fact Washington didn't win Yorktown at all. It was already won for him by the French, when de Grasse beat off the British fleet in Chesapeake Bay and when the French Army invested Gloucester, which forced Cornwallis to capitulate. Outside help, Lester! We wouldn't have a republic without it.'

'My God!'

'Ah hah!' Pip said and did a little dance. 'I knew that would get you.'

'It doesn't get me,' Terrada said. 'It escapes me. Any man who can rob Washington of Yorktown must be crazy or dangerous.'

'Well I'm not crazy,' Pip said, 'so that makes me dangerous.'

I walked away because I knew they would never settle it. I took some ice from the icebox to Judy, who had kept herself to the better half of the room with Hersey, White, Sam Salt, Wertenbaker, Phil Calhoun.

'I don't suppose I'll ever see you again,' Judy said to me as she dropped the ice like little anchors into the big glass jug. 'I mean when you leave.'

'I suppose not,' I said.

'Do you think you'll ever come back to America?'

'Why not?'

73

'You don't seem to have it in your eye. You haven't adapted yourself to America one tiny little bit, have you?'

'That's not true,' I said indignantly.

Judy shrugged. 'Anyway I guess Pip was right when he said you were wasting your time here.'

'I guess so.'

'I'll never understand the English. In fact Pip sometimes reminds me of an Englishman.'

I laughed. 'Don't tell him that.'

'I'm serious. I don't mean that Boston look about him, or rather that New England manner of his. It's something else.'

'Pre-revolutionary,' I suggested.

'What d'you mean?'

'A Continental Congress American?'

'No. No. He's more like those Americans who rushed off to help the English in 1914 in British uniforms, because they thought it their American duty. Pip's a little like that. He's got his own weird sense of an American's duty.'

I knew that Judy was pictorially right. Pip looked like a lightweight and behaved like one, but I could imagine him in a war in a tailored British uniform. His thin young American face and manner would emphasise the similarity rather than the difference, and I glanced at him across the room and felt a very strong affinity with Pip, an affection as well. He had now made it up with Terrada and they were laughing together over something.

'They'll always be together in all kinds of weather,' Judy said cynically and jealously.

'That's what friendship is,' I told her.

And that was how we broke it up for the war. Terrada left the next day for Washington and I spent my last two days on the 29th floor trying to anchor a restless, rootless Pip. Once, Judy put her head around the door and told me Pip was wandering around the corridors, 'lost without the other half of America. So why don't you take him downstairs to that ringside bar where you can watch the ice-skaters showing off their fat thighs and thick ankles.'

'Good idea,' I said and found Pip sitting in the room of

74

Miriam or Joan or Constance reading the AP despatches from Manila, which was expecting the Japanese invasion of Luzon any minute now.

'I don't know what the hell I'm doing here, Kit,' he said, an AP tear-off in his hand. 'I ought to be riding around the suburbs of Manila with MacArthur while he loses his underpants.'

I knew that someone called Teddy Johnson of the State Department had been ringing Pip since Pearl Harbor. But Pip said he had refused all requests to join his old China friends in government. 'I ain't a government man,' he said. 'Washington isn't my department.'

But it became Pip's department. When he came with Aimee and Judy to see me off at Penn Station he told me that the President had sent for him.

'That's terrific,' I said. 'And very flattering.'

'Yes,' Judy said. 'You and Lester will be able to put the two halves of America together again – one in the White House and the other in . . .'

In what?

We didn't know who Lester Terrada was working for in Washington.

'What about you?' I whispered teasingly in Judy's ear as I was about to get into the train. 'Which one is it going to be?'

'Wait and see,' she said.

But Judy had made her choice. Aimee and I embraced like a loving brother and sister. I loved Aimee. She wept a little and sniffed like a child over a family departure. She stood a little apart as Judy took Pip's arm possessively and waved on his behalf.

As I watched them standing there I suddenly felt sorry for Terrada. That curious, motherly sympathy for the man simply came over me and I couldn't help feeling again that he had been done out of his right. Instead of making a claim on Judy and a declaration of his manhood, he had allowed her to be very female about it and to brush him off in a sort of sexual test to see how much of a man he really was. He had failed. He had failed because he had been so surprised by

75

his initial success with Judy that he didn't know what to do next. Whereas it was easy for Pip to stand there with Judy's arm tucked into his.

I was tapped on the shoulder by the conductor as the train steamed out. He asked me to pull my head in. 'We lose a week's pay every time someone gets their head knocked off along here,' he said.

CHAPTER

7

That completed my brief education of Pip and Terrada at the time, and I felt that it was Pip's America I was leaving, not Terrada's.

A few months after I had left New York I received a telegram from Pip saying that he and Judy were married. I cabled back saying that I now looked forward to the arrival of a new generation of urban, immigrant Lovells, owing nothing to the Jackson-Jeffersonian tradition, although I knew that Judy wanted no truck with Pip's transmigrant theories. She was proud of her Anglo-Saxon family and had always accepted its American responsibilities.

A little while later I heard from Sam Salt that Pip and Terrada were deep in Washington politics, helping shape government policy on China and Russia. Sam said that they were as close and as far apart as they had ever been, which still puzzled me. If they were now in the real business of political decision how could they avoid an open break, or at least a violent disagreement?

Then one day when I was lying in a bomb hole on the side of a mountain in Tunisia waiting for some .88 shelling to stop (diverting myself with any old thought) I realised that these two would never split up until America itself split them up. In other words, their argument could only come to an end when America had finally chosen which way it was going, which history it was living by.

That didn't come for another seven or eight years. In the meantime I kept in touch with Pip and after the war when I went to live briefly in Cambridge, Massachusetts (I was using the Widener Library at Harvard) Pip and Judy would come north from Washington, bringing their pretty little urban baby with them.

'What did you call him?' I asked Pip when they first came.

'Lester . . .' Pip said apologetically.

I knew it wasn't his idea, it was Judy's.

I don't suppose I would have known much more than that if Aimee had not turned up as well. She had married a Navy flier, the boy she had once planned to knock down because he couldn't keep his hands off her. He had taken the GI Bill and was studying at Harvard Business School, and when Aimee found me through Pip she took me to a little café called the Oyster Bar just off Harvard Square and told me what had happened to her innocence.

'After you left,' she said, 'I changed my mind. I mean I wanted like mad for Judy to marry Lester because I wanted Pip myself. After a couple of weekends at the farm I wanted him awfully, Kit. I wanted to make him fall madly in love with me because I realised he was just like me – three-cylindered. I tried everything I could, only I was too fat and too clumsy, or my hair was awful, and I didn't know what to say to him. I was so dumb.'

I glanced at Aimee across the little plastic booth and wondered if Pip had realised what he was being offered. Aimee was still a little plump, but she was now a frank, lovely, womanish sort of woman, with all sorts of self-protections and a very delicate sort of sex buried deep under her hopelessly conventional clothes. She was trying to look like a matron before her time, and I felt sorry for Aimee because I knew it had all gone wrong somewhere.

'It was that damned boxing, Kit,' she said, inspecting me closely to make sure that I still understood and sympathised. 'You remember how I wanted to hit someone?'

'Yes,' I said. 'Lester.'

'No. No. I told you. I changed my mind about that. I wanted Lester to get Judy. Why don't you listen? It was the other boy.'

78

'I never met the other boy,' I pointed out.

'I know you didn't, but you will. Anyway, the next time he started to bother me I held out my left the way you taught me and hit him awfully hard with my right.'

I laughed, but I couldn't believe that this matronly young Aimee, this filled-out girl with a rather untidy edge to her expensive skirt would have done such a thing. 'I suppose he hit you back,' I said.

Aimee didn't laugh. 'That's exactly what he did do. I mean . . . it became a real fight. I lost my temper and just waded in, trying to smash him. In fact I went wild and he hit me hard, twice. To stop me, he said. Then I fell and he stood over me and I dove at his legs. It was awful, Kit, I'll never forget it. I was weeping and crying, and when I pulled him over it went all wrong. . . .'

I had not seen Aimee for four years and in the little Oyster Bar filled with students we were served with clam chowder and crackers, and I knew that Aimee had been saving this up to tell me. After all I was the only person who really knew how it had all started in that Connecticut barn.

'What do you mean – it went all wrong?' I asked her.

'Sex,' she said. 'It ended in sex. It was awful.'

I already knew one thing about this Aimee, I would have to be very gentle with her, so I said: 'It couldn't have been too bad. I mean you married the boy, didn't you? That was the one, wasn't it?'

'Yes, but I didn't want to. Not at first. I hated everything that happened that day, Kit. I can't tell you what it made me feel like. It wasn't ridiculous, like animals. It was . . . Oh I don't have to tell you. I got myself into such a bloody wet mess. I don't mean pregnant. Jack made a mess of me, that's all.'

Poor Aimee. Consummation for Aimee should have been a very delicate and flowerlike touch, safe in her own conventions of love and sex and marriage. Then it would have been rewarding on both sides. But Aimee was talking of violation, and what surprised me was that she still thought of it as violation.

'Then why on earth did you marry him?' I asked her.

'Well . . .' She sighed, and there was more in that sigh than in anything she said. 'Jack loved me, I suppose. He didn't at first. It was only after it happened. I don't think he could help doing what he did. That's the way most American men do it and think of it, Kit. I didn't think it was like that, but I suppose it has to be. Even the way they talk. He changed a bit afterwards. He came around like someone with a grievance against me, and I got to feeling that I owed him something. Isn't it funny? It was me who got to be in the wrong, so I just started doing what he wanted. I mean going here and there and playing the fool, and then when he went into the Navy I couldn't desert him, could I?'

My God, I thought, another convention ruining Aimee's life.

'So when he came back (he was wounded twice) I wouldn't let him touch me until we were married. And I suppose you'll laugh at me, Kit, but I didn't want anything. I honestly didn't. Not Jack or sex or anything. But we got married anyway, and' (Aimee looked all right but she had a way of weeping calmly as if she wasn't weeping at all) 'I suppose I thought marriage would make it different, but it didn't. Not really. Not the way I'm married anyway.'

I was embarrassed so I leaned across and took one of Aimee's rather plump hands and held it for a moment. 'Shush . . .' was all I could say.

'I know. I know. But it's all right.' She didn't wipe her eyes. She took a spoonful of her chowder and sniffed as she always did, like a child. 'But if it hadn't happened like that, if I'd had a little more time I might have persuaded Pip to look at me, because he and Judy didn't get on very well after you left. Did you know that Lester came back just after you left, before they were married, and tried to sweep Judy off her feet?'

'A likely story,' I said.

'I swear it. Someone in Washington must have told him where to buy some decent clothes, so he turned up on a Friday night in a new suit and wearing one of those big blousy ties that those awful senators from Georgia wear. He had a hat too. My God yes, a hat. He looked like Al Capone.'

'No, he didn't.'

'Yes, he did.'

'Was Pip there?'

'Of course he was. In fact I spent half the night watching Judy's bedroom door to see which one it was going to be. But by now I had this crush on Pip, so I was going to knock Pip down if he appeared. Honestly, I would have done it. But nothing happened, and the next day they had a big argument about Fenimore Cooper of all people. Lester and Judy ganged up on Pip, so I took Pip's side although I've forgotten what it was all about. Something to do with Cooper being too aristocratic – a patroon – because he didn't like Andrew Jackson. All I remember is that Pip said that no immigrant had the right to read Cooper, and I agreed with that because he's American, and people like Terrada oughtn't to claim they have any connection with Fenimore Cooper or even know anything about him.'

'You've got it wrong, Aimee,' I said gently.

'Maybe I have. I didn't know what it was about anyway. But I kept it going as long as I could because Judy began to be furious with Pip, which was great. Absolutely great. The trouble is that Terrada wasn't good enough, even for Judy. He just couldn't get anything going, not even with his hat on, which was sad for me, Kit, because if he had been a bit more of something, anything, I'm sure Judy would have married him instead of Pip even though she is a snob. But Lester was born spavined.'

I had forgotten exactly what spavined meant, but I knew what it did to horses. So Aimee was making a point which I didn't agree with. Lester had plenty going for him. His raw, physical attraction had always been more appealing to women than Pip's thin layer of argument and sex, and the only reason Aimee didn't feel physically attracted to Terrada was her dislike of any kind of animal attraction in man.

81

But she told me that Terrada tried again, this time in Washington. Judy had spent a week in their Aunt Felice's house in Chevy Chase, which she said was a suburb of Washington, and Lester had practically moved in on them. 'Although God knows where he got the gall from,' she said. 'Aunt Felice hated him although he thought she loved him because she's so damned polite.'

'What was Pip doing?'

'Nothing. Which is why Judy wanted him and got him. Judy's a horrible snob, Kit, and that clinched it as far as Pip was concerned. He didn't have a chance. She went down to Washington to get him and she got him. It was as simple as that. But I don't think Pip was very happy about it. He just gave in, the way I gave in to Jack. That's why we are alike. There's something missing in us. But they've never been happy, Kit, and I'm not happy either. In fact, I've discovered that nobody is supposed to be happy. I don't know anybody who is, so I guess Pip has made the most of it the way I do.'

Aimee may have been right, but my view of Pip at Cambridge was of a happy father who adored his baby son and indulged his wife in whatever disagreement or difference of opinion she had with him. He gave in as if he were willing to give in, and I must say that Judy extracted the full measure of her position. I remember on one of their first visits to us, she told my wife Eileen that I was a very sly Englishman and that when I was working for *Time* in New York I had hidden from everybody the fact that I was married. Pip (cocktail in hand because I had learned to make those martinis) tried to defend me, but Judy said:

'Don't lie. You were in it with him, and heaven knows what you two got up to when nobody was looking.'

'We got up to Staten Island, that's about all Kit and I ever got up to,' Pip said.

'I know all about that. But what about all that childish flirtation you both enjoyed with Aimee, and he made quite a thing of it after you left, Kit.'

'Let it go, Judy,' Pip said.

82

'Is Aimee the one Kit taught to box?' Eileen said. She hadn't met Aimee yet but she knew all about it.

'That's the one, my dear. They used to get up to all sorts of tricks in the big barn where we kept the horses.'

'I heard all about that,' Eileen said. 'Disgusting, wasn't it?'

Eileen was having a little fun with Judy. In fact Eileen was as strict with me as Judy was with Pip. But Eileen was a moral force, a Catholic who insisted on exclusiveness in all things. She was passionately loyal to her natural commitments – the family above all, so that anything Judy said about me would be dealt with on my behalf. She leaned over me as I poured another cocktail in our Linnaean Street flat and whispered: 'She's mean, isn't she,' and knowing that Eileen would take sides openly if she felt like it, I whispered back Pip's advice: 'Let it go. It's not important.' Which seemed to be Pip's attitude to almost everything Judy said.

Aimee told me one more thing. When Judy joined Pip in Washington, after their marriage, they lived near Aunt Felice in an old apartment block owned by Aunt Felice, and below Lester Terrada. 'Judy made damn sure that Lester was always around somewhere. She always wanted both men, and my God, in Washington she almost had both of them.'

In fact, one of the reasons that Pip and Judy came north to Cambridge was to see Lester Terrada, who was a visiting lecturer (instructor) in a half course which Harvard had arranged for its graduate students in Postwar American Politics. Lester seemed to be preparing himself for a possible academic appointment, and Pip too seemed to be on the same route. I don't know why Terrada had thought of it, perhaps it was something to do with his background, but Pip had been very upset by Roosevelt's death and he didn't have much rapport with President Truman, so he was looking around for another outlet. Both of them were in that difficult moment between war and peace, the only difference being that Pip seemed to be sulking in his

83

Washington tent, whereas Terrada was still in full battle array and following the drums and fifes of the Truman administration.

Inevitably, I saw and spoke with Lester, and I suppose our brief meetings in Cambridge, Mass., should have prepared me for what happened later, except that I was not looking that far ahead. At the time it was more of a pleasant interlude. After all we were all young and recently married – Eileen and myself, Pip and Judy, Aimee and her Navy flier, Jack. The war was over, life suddenly had an open end to it, and our futures were like a pavement being laid stone by stone, day by day, on the way to somewhere. I loved the interlude and so did Eileen.

But Eileen was too cautious and suspicious to make friends with Judy or Terrada. She got on well with Aimee and with Pip, and I got on well with all of them, even with the outsider Jack (Aimee's husband), who seemed out of place anywhere but in a Navy mess hall. Jack's hair was still short, his schoolboyish eyes were restless, and he was never quite with us. Almost everything he said began with 'Hey, you guys.' Probably because he longed to be where the guys were. I liked him for it because he was not aware of it; but whenever he spoke to Aimee he seemed curiously detached, as if marriage was a rather impersonal affair, not to be confused with normal Navy behaviour.

Without knowing it we had thus created a little knot in Cambridge society, and it was here that I began to see the first signs of the coming division of America, the split that would divide Pip and Lester into opposite camps. It was already obvious that it would be men like Lester who would take charge of American affairs, whereas freaks like Pip were about to be discarded. But what we couldn't foresee was the extent to which the division would take place, and how brutally the discarded would be dealt with. I think Pip knew what was coming and in defiance of it he played games with his attitude, which was his way of not giving in to the mood of the times. And in the long run that was enough to bring him down.

84

8

On the other hand Lester was one of the Americans of the 'American century', and the first sign I saw of the split between them was not so much the result of an argument, but a difference in their attitudes to a situation that became a witch-hunt in embryo and would end several years later with the suicide of its victim – Professor F. O. Matthiessen.

I knew Matthiessen only slightly. He was an established Professor of English at Harvard and I was a young man from nowhere. But both Pip and Terrada knew him well, and for me the incident began one day when I was working in one of the two dusty little rooms that Professor Theodore Spencer kept for his tutorials almost opposite the Harvard main gate, on a first floor above a dress shop. Ted Spencer let me use his study and I was dreaming by the window when I heard a student in the next room say to Spencer in a worried voice:

'Say, Professor, d'you think it's really true that F. O. Matthiessen is a communist? I mean is it true that he gives everything a Marxist slant? I mean is all that stuff on Dreiser right or wrong? I'd really like to know what's up before I switch to his course.'

I wondered for a moment what Ted Spencer would say. Spencer was an Elizabethan scholar, but he was also a friend to all poets and writers no matter what their politics. He had just returned from Florida where he had been sent by the Justice Department to pass judgment on the sanity of Ezra Pound, who had been sent home under close arrest as a traitor after spending the war in Italy and broadcasting for the Italians. 'Ezra is as sane as he ever was,' Spencer had told me, 'and that says a lot for Ezra because he never claimed to be more than half sane about anything. So if he wants to plead insanity I'll go along with it.' That was a declaration for Ezra Pound accused of being a fascist, so I waited to see what he would say about F. O. Matthiessen accused of being a Marxist, and by implication a communist and a dangerous influence.

'It's no use asking me to say anything about another professor,' I heard Spencer say very evenly. 'And anyway I'm not here to give you advice on any course but my own. So don't ask me questions like that.'

'Yes, but I thought you might give me a hint. . . .'

'No hints, no comments, no advice. You'll have to make up your own mind about Professor Matthiessen's course.'

I wasn't surprised by the conversation, because Harvard then was very rich in young men who were only half-formed adults, even though they had been well-formed soldiers. The coffee booths were full of them and they were all asking nervous questions about life because their competitive futures were at stake, and they didn't want to go off somewhere in the wrong intellectual direction. But the intellectual direction of the true academy was something else, and for those who were worried about it the defence of Matthiessen meant more than the stumbling future of a thousand hungry young men. For those of us who knew Matthiessen, the idea that this gentle, fragile man, who was a perfect academic and a devoted teacher, the idea that he was a dangerous influence was not only untrue, it was cruel and stupid. Yet that was in the air. And though it was difficult to trace, or even identify what was happening, Matthiessen knew he was under attack. So did the students. And of course so did Pip and Terrada.

Maybe it would have been nothing more than one of their usual disagreements if Pip hadn't made a little gesture of it. It was a weekend. Pip and Judy had come up to Boston to see a publisher who wanted Pip to write a book on

America's China policy. But I think Pip was still making his off-hand presence felt among the Harvard gentry. In any case he stayed as usual with one of the professors from the Oriental languages department a few doors from us in Linnaean Street. I don't know what Lester was doing in Cambridge this time. He always came and went importantly and (it seemed to me) mysteriously, as if he had some semi-secret link with the Harvard faculty that ought not to be explained; unlike Pip, who always appeared to be doing something so simple and casual that it was hardly worth mentioning.

Eileen had prepared one of her elaborate suppers – elaborate because after a wartime of rationing where we had come from, America offered a sudden explosion of food which couldn't be resisted. She was an enthusiastic cook and both Pip and Terrada were enthusiastic eaters so they came at the table from opposite ends as if they would demolish it between them. It pleased the cook and we were fat and happy, although there was a thunderstorm in a snowstorm outside which made us rush to the window of the apartment to watch a ball of fire bouncing off the local public school opposite.

F. O. Matthiessen dropped into our conversation like everything else concerned with Harvard: college gossip, college rivalries and college politics were our daily fare. Pip said his publisher knew about Matthiessen's life-long interest in Theodore Dreiser, and they wanted Matthiessen to switch publishers and give them the definitive study of Dreiser he was working on.

'They'd be crazy if they did that,' Lester said.

'Why?' Pip asked him.

'Because Matty has become a copy of Dreiser himself, in fact he admits it, and that's bound to colour his book and discredit Matty himself.'

'Why, in God's name, should it do that?' Pip wanted to know.

'Dreiser was a communist,' Terrada said.

'So?'

'Matty's a teacher, Pip. He ought to be more responsible.'

'Why? Isn't he a good teacher?'

'That's not the point,' Terrada said.

'Oh! Oh! And Oh again,' Pip said. 'So what is the point?'

'Matty's allowing his politics to get the better of him. He's going too far. He should keep out of politics.'

'Keeping out of politics is a way of putting yourself into them. Leaving the old status quo.'

'But it's a fundamental principle that's at stake,' Terrada boomed. 'An academic principle at that.'

'What academic principle?'

'There has to be a limit to a teacher's commitment outside teaching,' Terrada muttered and he was deeply concerned, he was very serious, he was troubled.

'That's the most horrific thing I've heard since the Scopes evolution case,' Pip said. 'What limit? Who's going to decide the limits? It's un-Greek. It's un-American, Lester.'

'Oh don't be silly, Pip,' Judy said. 'Lester's right. Matty should watch his step. That's all he's saying.'

'You need more consideration than that to justify the attacks on Matty,' Pip said drily.

So far it was no more than an academic argument – metaphorically speaking anyway. We had a pleasant evening and Eileen was very pleasant to Judy although Judy (try as she might) couldn't come to grips with Eileen. Eileen's thin skin always became impervious whenever someone attempted to penetrate it.

A few days later, quite by coincidence, Pip and Terrada and I were lunching at the Harvard Club. I was lunching with Ted Spencer, eating their horse-meat steak for bravado rather than taste, and Pip and Terrada were eating alone. They joined us, and after a certain amount of gossip about the academics who had been enthusiastic New Dealers and had rushed off to Washington to help Roosevelt but were now drifting back to the colleges, Pip said: 'Look. There's Matty, eating alone. Why don't I go over and get him?'

It was hardly a question, rather a suggestion. But I was surprised when Terrada leaned back in his chair and said, 'I wouldn't do that if I were you.'

Pip was also surprised. 'I hope that doesn't mean what I think it means,' he said to Terrada.

'I don't want to eat with him, that's all it means.'

'You mean you're still in government, so you don't want to be seen talking to him,' Pip said.

'Okay. And I'm still in government and I don't want to be seen talking to him. Nor should you.'

'For Christ's sake,' Pip said, picking up his plate and pushing back his chair. 'If we can't have him over here, I'm going over there.'

I was with Spencer, so I waited to see what he would do. Ted sat still. It wasn't his quarrel, so there was no reason for him to do anything. Lester, Spencer and I finished the meal in a very subdued mood, and when it was time to go Lester walked out without saying anything to Pip or Matthiessen. Spencer greeted Matty and talked with him for a moment, and I sat down with them to take an extra cup of coffee.

I don't know if Matthiessen realised what was going on. He was a quiet man and he listened politely to Pip explaining why Anne Boleyn's family had been very important to Tudor England. 'They're the most underestimated influence on Henry's reign,' Pip said. 'They wanted total Nonconformist reform of church and state and if Anne had been Queen long enough the reformation in England might have gone much farther than it did, which is why Henry cut her head off. He didn't want it to go that far.'

'It couldn't have got much farther at the time,' Matthiessen said. 'After all, it took another hundred years for any popular dissent to show itself in England.'

'Because it didn't have any direction or leadership,' Pip said. 'Which is what the Boleyn family were secretly giving it.'

They went on discussing it until their coffee got cold, and when Pip and I parted with Matthiessen and walked across the square in the light blue snow, Pip said rather savagely:

'I wonder why the bastards are so afraid of Matty. He's not even a Marxist, goddam it, which shouldn't make any difference anyway. All Matty cares about is the good old American tradition of social criticism in the novel, and if they're going to pick him up on that, Kit, God knows where it will end. Some day we'll be locked up for reading Jack London, or even Mark Twain.'

'It isn't that bad,' I said to cheer him up. 'Not yet, anyway.'

'Don't be so damn sure,' Pip said gloomily. 'The longer I sit around Washington, the more scared I get. I thought the colleges might be better, but it looks as if it's happening here too, which is maybe more frightening.'

'Oh, the Areopagus is always being threatened,' I said with a shrug.

'Yeah . . . .' Pip said. 'By Lester?'

Yet they didn't seem deeply affected by it. All through that November and December I saw Judy and Pip and Terrada whenever they came up to Cambridge; and once we went south to Washington and stayed in a hotel (owned by Aunt Felice) not far from the apartment block where they all lived. Because we were then childless, Eileen and I made a fuss of little Lester who was a silent and curiously resentful baby, quite unlike Pip in appearance except maybe for his slow-blinking eyes.

'He'll grow up to look like Lester,' Eileen said. 'Pompous.'

Eileen was cold-blooded about all three of them and she tried to convince me they were three rivals rather than three friends.

'Nonsense,' I said. 'They only seem a bit odd [I didn't mean physically odd] because Judy is in the middle, while Pip and Terrada still go on behaving as if she isn't there at all.'

'You're quite wrong,' she said. 'It's Judy who keeps them together. She's the cart and they're the horses.'

'Now don't be too hard on them,' I said. 'After all, they are my friends.'

90

'Then don't get sentimental about them,' Eileen replied. 'Pip knows exactly what's happening but he doesn't seem to be able to do anything about it.'

'What d'you mean . . . *he knows what's happening*?'

'He knows he's a horse,' Eileen said.

'He doesn't behave like a horse.'

'Oh, yes he does. He goes exactly where Judy wants him to go. He's nice, Kit, but he's rather weak.'

'What about Lester?'

'Him too.'

'In that case they're two weak horses going in different directions,' I pointed out.

'Oh, Pip goes off on his own sometimes. But she brings him back. It was Aimee who told me that Pip is a different person when he's alone, but I've never seen him without Judy or Lester so I wouldn't know. But maybe she's right.'

I realised that I too hadn't seen Pip alone for more than five minutes. I had reported the incident in the Harvard Club to Eileen, but she was less impressed with it than I had been. In fact I began to watch all three with Eileen's suspicious green eyes, and I began to feel sorry for Pip. Only occasionally would he take up a good, weird, theoretical attitude, or show any of his marvellous insight into what *is*. Eileen said: 'Look at his eyes, they're sad.' So they were, or rather Pip no longer looked out. He seemed to be looking in, and he must have groomed himself to be conventional. He wore thin ties and drain-pipe trousers and you could picture this Pip sitting in some Washington office, going through his documents, making his reports, lunching with his executive colleagues and keeping his own counsel in public like any good government man. But every now and then he would say something which made a little mockery of it.

'Old Kit!' he said to me quietly as we walked fifty yards behind Eileen and Judy and Lester down Linnaean Street. 'The trouble with you, old man, is that you don't say enough. You really ought to pick up Lester when he talks like that.'

91

Lester had been telling us at dinner how the United States would not only keep its forces in Europe but would have to remain there for at least fifty years, not simply to contain communism but to give the flaccid population of Europe a moral backbone which they seemed to lack in themselves.

'I expected *you* to argue with him,' I said to Pip. 'After all, you're in government so you're the expert.'

'Don't be so damned cynical,' Pip said to me with a little of his old bite. 'What you should have done was to remind Lester of the days when he was so bloody determined to keep the United States out of Europe. Out of anywhere in fact.'

'Why didn't you remind him?' I said.

'I don't remind anybody of anything any more.'

'Why not?'

'Marital bliss, Kit, sometimes depends on a bad memory.'

It was the only time he made any overt reference to his marriage and I didn't ask him more about it because I didn't want to spoil my record – minding my own business. I also knew that if he wanted to tell me more he would.

This was true also of his work in Washington. He never talked about it but once, and that was when we were finally sitting alone together in the Oyster Bar. He told me that he was going to China after Christmas and it would probably be his last trip on government business.

When I asked him why, he said: 'Because I don't know what my business is any more. You can't make a policy out of facts, Kit. Not these days. U.S. China policy is now in the fat little hands of the Generalissimo's lobby in Congress, and pretty soon it'll shift to the House Committee on Un-American Activities. So there's no place left for anyone who knows what is really going on in China.'

'What *is* going on in China, Pip?' I asked him. 'You never talk about it.'

'The communists are going on. What else?'

'Aren't you supposed to be trying to stop them?'

Pip laughed. 'Nothing's going to stop them. China's

about to be turned over like an old sod. Five hundred years of corruption and misery are about to be buried, and if the United States had any sense we'd go along with it instead of listening to those silly bastards in Congress and government who'll support anybody, no matter how corrupt, so long as they hate the reds. It's a stupid policy, Kit, and it's going to end up in a very dirty war somewhere. It's bound to. So I want to get out of the way before that happens.'

'You're actually quitting?'

'Yes. But don't say anything to Judy. I haven't told her yet.'

'What about Lester? Does he know?'

Pip seemed to hesitate. He slowed his step and swung his hands wide as if to expand his chest or to warm himself. He hated the cold, he was too thin to enjoy it. 'Lester and I keep off the subject of personal commitments these days,' he said.

'That's a hell of a situation,' I said.

Pip held me back as we almost caught up with the others. 'Just a minute, Kit. I want to tell you something,' he said.

We stood for a moment on the pavement. Then he took my arm and we walked on slowly so that our conversation did not seem too private or too deliberate.

'I don't want to push my friendship with Lester into a hopeless corner,' he said seriously. 'So don't ask me too many questions about it.'

'Okay,' I said, and apologised for being inquisitive.

'It's not that,' he said. 'I don't want to make an issue of anything these days, particularly anything about myself. Not with Lester anyway. Pretty soon the only thing that people like me will be able to count on is friendship, so I don't want to make it too hard on Lester.'

'I understand,' I said.

'Maybe you do, and maybe you don't. But it's not a situation I can do much about,' he said, and by then we were too near the others to continue.

But as I walked back that night, with Eileen on my arm, I was thinking again about this odd friendship and how much

93

Pip had invested in it and how much he depended on it. It was still a puzzle, because Pip always seemed to make it a duty, as if he always owed something to Lester Terrada which was worth a great deal of toleration and understanding. But what was it?

I think I guessed that night that I would never really know. I was pretty sure that I was right about one aspect of it: that Pip wanted the Terradas of the great republic to know what they'd got, and who they were. Not to be pale copies of two hundred colonial English revolutionaries, but a people with a new destiny of their own which should begin with themselves, and not as a memory of a farming backwoods community with an immense frontier before them.

'All right,' I told myself. 'All that is understood. But what is going to happen now that Pip's under real pressure? What is he protecting the friendship for? Does he really believe it is all that valuable?'

I didn't know; but one thing I had forgotten – that I too was a friend. It was Aimee who reminded me, when I saw her, that I was also important to Pip, although I suppose I had always known it without thinking about it.

'You're not an American, Kit,' she said, 'and Pip counts on that to keep you out of trouble. I mean, he thinks that pretty soon anyone who's a close friend of his is going to be accused of something awful. I think he's crazy. He's exaggerating. But he told me only the other day that you're one of the few people who understands what he's talking about and isn't scared stiff by staring a situation in the face, whatever that means. But he needs someone like you, so why do you have to go? Why don't you stay here and become an American citizen?'

I was lunching with Aimee at the Oyster Bar, and I had been telling her that I would return to England in three weeks' time.

'I've finished here,' I told her. 'No reason for me to stay on, and no reason to become an American citizen.'

'Why not? What's the matter with becoming an American citizen?'

94

'Nothing. Excepting that I'm English, Aimee. That's all.'

'Well, I wish you'd stay.'

'Why are you so worried?' I asked her. 'Pip's all right.'

'I know he is. But I have this awful bloody feeling that he's going to need all the friends he can get.'

I said I knew all about that too. 'But he'll be all right. Judy'll look after him.'

I said it as provocation for Aimee knowing what she thought of Judy.

But Aimee didn't rise to it. 'How on earth can you eat this stuff,' she said and pushed her fish soup away.

I told her that it was the best fish soup I had ever tasted.

'Well, I'm getting fat anyway, ever since I gave up riding. And anyway this really is a godawful place, Kit. Why do you come here? As for Judy and Pip and me and everybody else, you know very well that it's all gone wrong and that nobody is in the right place any more and never will be. So don't talk to me about Judy and Pip. I hate Judy and she hates me, and God help Pip if he ever really needs her.'

I was sorry then that I had teased her, and my memory of our parting has always been spoiled by my silly provocation, because I had forgotten about Aimee's own situation and was only thinking of Pip and Judy and their problems.

9

Pip was not a good correspondent. Neither was I. So our letters were usually brief, kidding notes that reported a few general facts about work and family and a few sour comments on the state of the world, but otherwise nothing very revealing about ourselves. Even so I knew what was happening to Pip because I knew what was happening to America. I could read it every day in the papers.

Pip wrote that he had abandoned Washington after his China trip and that he was now concentrating on finishing his book about America's China policy. He had moved into a little white house in Brookline, Mass., and he had been lecturing fairly regularly on the China question and Pacific policies at various universities: Dartmouth, Chicago, Southern California, Columbia, Princeton, Harvard and his old alma mater – Yale – etc. That lasted about a year. Then he told me that four out of five universities said they no longer wanted him, and three had asked him to sign a declaration that he was not a communist and did not support communism in China.

Pip had refused. 'I know what I'm not,' he said. 'and I'm not a communist. But when they start making you swear what you are or what you are not, that's the end.' He wouldn't do it. He did add in a postscript that this had got him into trouble with Lester, who not only signed similar declarations himself but advocated them as requirements for all men in public life.

Even so, Pip still made excuses for Lester. 'He's still in the administration, so he hasn't much choice,' Pip wrote. 'But what he doesn't understand is that these self-denunciations, these loyalty oaths, are contrary to a dozen declarations in the Constitution which Lester puts so much store on. When I point out that he believes in the Constitution only when it suits him and then denies it when he disagrees with it, he practically takes off. He thinks I'm playing into the hands of the communists. And that's when I despair, Kit. You've read what's happening here, but whatever you read it's a damn sight worse than you think.'

What I was reading were the daily despatches from Korea about the war, and the daily despatches from New York and Washington about the hunt for communists in the holes and corners of American life. Two months later Pip wrote a sad little note saying that he and Owen Lattimore (another Pacific policy expert) were being attacked in the various Congressional committees and subcommittees. 'But even the Boy Scouts are being accused of communism,' he said, 'so nobody's going to escape. The McCarthy and McCarran committees are after American blood and they're hunting down (and imprisoning if they can) actors, writers, teachers, newspapermen, priests and anybody from the old Roosevelt crowd they can label. Hysteria, Kit, is becoming an American way of life.'

I wrote back telling Pip that we had similar though less dangerous symptoms in Europe, but I suggested that he would be better off in England so why didn't he pack up and come over? Eileen and I could put them up if need be.

There was no reply from Pip and I guessed that the situation had finally caught up with him. In fact I had to read in *The Times* that Philip Lovell, a former Roosevelt adviser on China affairs, had been named as a communist agent by Lester Terrada, another adviser to the Roosevelt administration. There was not much information from the *Times* report; it simply said that while being questioned as a witness before a Senate subcommittee on another matter, Lester Terrada had named Lovell as one of the policy-makers who had influenced Roosevelt's Pacific policies in

97

favour of Chinese communism – policies which were inimical to United States interests.

'I can't believe it!' I told Eileen stupidly as I read it aloud over breakfast. 'I simply can't believe it.'

'Then you must be naive or stupid,' Eileen said. 'I'm surprised it didn't happen before.'

'Even so . . .'

I knew the kind of trouble Pip would be in now so I wrote repeating my offer, and about a month later he wrote back telling me what had happened. 'It's no use trying to write a neat, coherent letter about it,' he said, 'because I'm not a coherent person at the moment, and I'm not likely to be for some time. So don't expect too much from me. I'm sitting in a room in Aunt Felice's hotel in Washington trying to sort out what's happening to me here. You want to know how Lester could have done it? Well, I'll tell you how he did it, Kit. The stupid bastard trapped himself into it, so that betraying me was the only way out for him.'

'There he goes again,' I said to Eileen. 'Excuses for Lester.' But I read on.

'You know what it was like just before you left. Argument and discussion between people like Lester and me were no longer a search for an answer but a declaration of intention. That's Washington language for choosing sides, although it probably doesn't mean a damn thing to you. But I didn't think he'd do it, Kit. They had him by the balls because they knew about his youthful excursions to Russia, and Lester was a communist at some time or another. So he was cold meat for the committees, particularly since he was still in the administration. So he had to do one of two things: he either had to prove his loyalty by denouncing me when they questioned him about me, or he had to go to the wall himself.'

The result was obvious.

'Do you know what Lester said when he read my book, Kit? He said, "You've gone wrong on America, Pip, because your book is straight communist propaganda and somebody ought to put you right."

'So we had a flaming row and you can imagine what state we were in when he began making his pronouncements to the Senate subcommittee. Even so, I didn't expect him to name me, Kit, even though they asked him direct questions about me, and even though I had already been named by a couple of professional informers before the McCarran Committee. But what that bastard Lester did was to make it personal knowledge of my attitude, so now they've recalled him and they're going to insist on a lot more. Which means he has to retract what he said about me, or go on proving my guilt. And I give you one guess, Kit, what he'll do, because Lester's only started to squeal.'

There was another long silence from Pip after that and I knew he was in too much trouble to reply to my letters. But I knew from the English papers that Terrada's first words of denunciation had inevitably become a torrent of damning recollection. Day after day Terrada recalled almost every attitude Pip had taken in their endless arguments. He re-called every incident that revealed Pip's un-American point of view. Five years of friendship with Pip became five years of evidence against him, and some of the most damning of it was Pip's attitude to the Jacksonian 'myths' and his 'contempt' for the founding fathers and the Constitution.

Not only was Pip revealed as a supporter of Chinese communism, but in a week of testifying, Terrada had somehow re-created a man so committed to wider subversive philosophies and dangerous political attitudes that he, Terrada, finally had to declare that the years of their friendship had really been years of trying to counter the effect that these dangerous ideas would have if they were allowed to go unchallenged.

Terrada had challenged Phillip Lovell's ideas until he realised it was hopeless. So he was now putting the problem to the Senate committee in the hope that they could do what he, Terrada, had failed to do. And Terrada said in his last statement that he had appeared before this committee not only for the good of America but for the good of Phillip Lovell and others like him who needed to be shown why

99

their attitudes were not only dangerous and wrong but fundamentally un-American and subversive.

I wondered of course how Pip was taking it, and I probably would never have known if Aimee had not turned up one bright spring day in London. She had come to Europe with her husband Jack for a three-week Easter vacation, and while Jack went off to see an uncle in Germany, Aimee came over to London, 'Because,' she said, 'I'm a damn sight more Anglo- than German-Saxon.'

Aimee waited until we were alone in our London flat (Eileen was busy in the kitchen) before she began to tell me about herself, and eventually about Pip. 'Don't ask about me, Kit,' she said when I wanted to know how she was. 'I'm a permanent disaster area, and I'll never be anything else.'

When I raised my metaphorical eyebrow and asked why, she said: 'I'm so damn sorry now that I didn't stick to horses. Horses can be human but some men can't help being animals. Oh, I don't mean tooth and claw and foot and mouth. I mean other things. I hate sex. I wish God had made some other way for a man to be a man, and a woman to be a woman. Anyway, that's enough about me. It's Pip I'm worried about.'

She said that Pip was almost on his own now. 'Judy's on Lester's side. She wants Pip to give in and sign all those loyalty oaths they keep putting in front of him. But Pip says he's loyal enough without signing anything and I believe him, Kit. I'll never believe that Pip is a subversive, no matter what Lester Terrada and a lot of those drunken Congressmen say. I don't know what's happening in Washington, but whatever it is I'm on Pip's side, even though nobody else is at the moment. Particularly Judy.'

'But what's happening?' I asked her. 'I mean between him and Judy.'

'They quarrel all the time. The last time she wanted to invite Terrada over to talk with Pip. But Pip said he'd walk out if Terrada ever walked in. Ever again. He never wanted to see the awful bastard again. Pip's like me. Once he's in

100

something he's in it. That's his trouble. And that's why he'll never leave Judy. Never.'

When I asked her how Pip was – in his Lovell soul – she said: 'How do you expect him to be? He was calm at first, but the worse it gets the madder Pip gets. And now he's just waiting for them to put him on the stand again so he can say a few things about Lester Terrada and about the Senate committee too.'

I told Eileen afterwards what Aimee had said and she called Pip a fool. 'He should have married Aimee,' she said. 'Aimee would have stuck by him through thick and thin, even though she doesn't seem to know what's going on.'

'I wonder about that,' I said.

'Wonder about what?'

'If Aimee doesn't know what's going on. She may not understand politics but she certainly has her own ideas about Washington. She says everything that's happening there is disgusting.'

Aimee had told me that Washington was like a brothel. 'Honestly! When I see all those Senators and Congressmen they all look like men who are visiting prostitutes. They've got that look in their faces. Going into places or coming out.'

'How do you know what men look like when they're going into those places and coming out?' I asked her.

'I'm a woman and I know. They're awful. Everything they're doing is awful. I don't believe anything they say. I'd sooner believe Pip, whatever he says, and sometimes he says some stupid things. But it's a good thing you didn't stay, Kit. We must look awful.'

We saw Aimee off at Heathrow when Jack came over from Germany to pick her up on the way home. Jack was friendly and kidding, and he said to Eileen as we waited for their baggage to be weighed in: 'Isn't she a real little Momma?' He pointed at Aimee as if Aimee were two blocks away.

'She's lovely,' Eileen replied, and as I looked at Aimee I knew that both of them were right. Aimee had locked her body in the stiff foundations and iron curves of what was then the New Look. She wore a small blue hat with a white veil around it and carried net gloves, and though her clothes were obviously expensive she looked like a small-town housewife decked out to visit her local women's club. Two tears made perfect little furrows down her make-up as she embraced us both, and I realised that no matter what Aimee did to herself she couldn't hide her innocent beauty, which seemed more innocent as she grew older.

'She's lost weight,' I said as they walked through the immigration doors and out of sight.

'She's lost something else too,' Eileen said.

'What?'

'I don't know, Kit. Something to do with being a woman.'

I knew what it was, and it was not something lost. Aimee was still being cheerfully violated by the man she considered the typical American male, and I suspected that Aimee was beginning to feel the lasting effects of 'grinning and bearing it'. That was what Eileen's feminine feelers had detected through Aimee's ridiculous clothes and absurd hat, but she didn't realise it.

The day after Aimee left I finally heard from Pip, not a letter but a copy of his book *The Future of China-American Relations*, and I hurried through it to try and find some of the clues to his dilemma.

In fact the book was no more than a very objective study of what was happening in China. Pip's theory was the one he had always believed in – that four or five powerful banking families ruled China, and that traditional corruption, exploitation and feudal brutalities had seeped right through every stratum of the society, leaving the urban masses and the millions of starving peasants with no recourse but to support the communist revolutionaries. Like Edgar Snow and other Americans Pip presented this condition as a fact, not as an attitude. The future of China, he said, was obviously and inevitably communist, and that was what the United States would have to come to terms

102

with if it wanted to retain some links with future, mainland China.

It was not an unusual analysis even then, but what was unusual was Pip's concluding chapter in which he predicted what was going to happen in the future, but which seemed ridiculous at the time. Pip said that, whatever the short term American policy, in the long run America would inevitably align herself with communist China as a counterbalance to the Russians. Moreover the Chinese communists themselves would look for an American alliance, because their kind of peasant and rather petty-bourgeois and narrowly national (Pip's words) communism was not like the Russian kind, and inevitably it would come into conflict with conventional western or Soviet Marxism. It would be this that would bring capitalist America and communist China together, and though he didn't like the idea (personally he preferred the Russians as allies) it was inevitable.

This came up in a later session of the hearings when one of the committee questioned Pip on this aspect of his book. Pip's reply was not very helpful. 'I'm not advocating it,' he said. 'I'm simply telling you what will happen. And you, Senator, if you are still alive, will probably be the first to welcome such a policy.'

In fact the Senator did become one of the early admirers of the new China policy more than twenty years later, but in that committee hearing the Senator lost his temper with Pip and told him he would be held in contempt of Congress if he persisted in implying future communist sympathies to members of the committee.

'You're the one who is here to answer for your loyalty,' the Senator said, 'not members of this committee.'

'Nonetheless . . .' was all Pip managed to shout back.

What the committee did in effect was not only use Pip's book as proof of Pip's communist sympathies, but they countered everything Pip said in his own defence with some damning fragment taken from Terrada's recollections of their friendship. Additionally, two informers who were former communists appeared before the committee to

103

claim that in Communist Party meetings Phillip Lovell had been spoken of as a 'progressive and sympathetic influence' in the White House, and that when his book appeared it was sold widely in Communist Party bookshops as a friendly document, a repetition of what other informers had already said about Owen Lattimore's books.

After another two weeks of Congressional inquisition it was obvious that in his five years at the White House Pip's influence on American policy had been subversive, un-American and communist-inspired; and despite the recall of Terrada to the stand by Pip's lawyers, despite some sharp questions and heated exchanges, when the committee finally adjourned it looked as if the Justice Department would summon Pip before a federal grand jury to answer some sort of charge that would be prepared by the Attorney General.

In effect Pip had now been officially branded a traitor.

CHAPTER

10

In the months that followed, Pip's case slowly drifted into a legal tangle as his lawyers used precedent and constitutional law to keep it from coming before a federal grand jury. But I managed to get a reply from Pip even though he never wrote more than a few lines to tell me what was happening. He was bitter. But there was no sign of self-pity or panic, even though his life was now in ruins. No one would employ him. He had been denounced by churches, newspapers, veterans' organisations and politicians. His book had been banned in almost every public library in the United States, and it had been burned outside a public library in Milwaukee. He had been knocked down by two men in Boston, and the owner of the house he had rented in Brookline had gone to the local court and achieved an injunction forbidding him to enter the house, even though his tenancy was still contractually valid.

He never mentioned Terrada or Judy or his son, but in a postscript to one letter he mentioned Aimee affectionately and said: 'They're living in New York, and I think she's trying to renew her love affair with the horse. She's taken to wearing jodhpurs and she's cut her hair short.'

'What did I tell you?' Eileen said when she read it.

'Well, I hope it works,' I said.

It didn't work because one Sunday morning when Jack was playing squash at some rackets club or other, Aimee committed suicide.

'She didn't leave any kind of note to explain; or rather

Jack hasn't found one,' Pip wrote. 'But Jack said that though they had been quarrelling it was no more than usual. Before she cut her wrists in the bathroom,' Pip went on, 'Aimee took a hammer and smashed every plate in their New York apartment. She put them all on the living room floor and smashed them one by one. Nothing else. Just the plates. Which needs some explaining, Kit, like those damned, bloody, stupid horses.'

That was all, except perhaps a revealing sentence at the end. 'Don't write and ask me for details because you won't get any. I'm just not talking about it.'

Pip then added a few lines about himself. He said he was still fighting an indictment, and he was about to sue Lester Terrada for libel or defamation in a Washington court. 'They didn't give me a chance at him in the committee hearings,' he said, 'so I'll get him in a civil court. Everybody tells me I haven't a hope in hell of winning the case, but at least I'll be able to expose the bastard as a hypocrite, a liar and a paid informer. (After all, he's getting his reward isn't he?)'

I felt at the time that the information in Pip's letter about Aimee was so thin that it seemed cold-blooded. In fact I was so upset by Aimee's death and so bothered by it that for a while I decided that I was taking it harder than Pip. Later Pip would correct that impression, but in the meantime Eileen wept a little, saying: 'Poor Aimee. Poor kid!' and I wandered around asking myself why in God's name had she done it, until Eileen became annoyed and said:

'All right. All right. Why did she do it?'

I didn't want to be clever, but I believed that I knew the answer, and perhaps stupidly responded too crudely. 'Aimee was violated just once too often,' I said.

'Oh, nonsense!' Eileen replied. 'That doesn't explain why she killed herself.' And being more practical Eileen looked for a lost alternative. 'If only Pip had taken up with Aimee and walked out on Judy.'

It was an alternative I had always wanted for them myself, and the idea became even more poignant a few months later when I read in *Time* magazine that Judy had walked out on Pip.

Judy had announced it at a meeting organised by the Daughters of the American Revolution, which she was addressing in Washington. Like Lester, she told the story of her fruitless attempts to change Pip's thinking from subversive and dangerous ideas to normal and acceptable Americanism. She said she was leaving him not only for the good of America but for the good of her son, and the boy's future as an American. There could be no future for little Lester as long as his father refused to declare himself (sign himself) a loyal American, and renounce his pro-communist sympathies.

'I hope he shoots her,' Eileen said.

'More likely someone is going to shoot Pip.'

'Then he ought to get out of America,' Eileen said. 'Even for a little while.'

'They wouldn't let him go.'

'He could sneak out somehow.'

'What'd be the use of that? Even if he got here I doubt if the British authorities would let him stay.'

'Why don't you write and ask him anyway?' Eileen suggested.

I did, and it was another letter that Pip did not answer. In fact Pip stopped writing altogether and thereafter I had to follow his case in the press. I heard nothing at all of his libel suit against Terrada, and much later I would learn that he couldn't find an attorney who would present his case for him, not even the loyal attorney who was fighting his indictment for him. Slowly Pip began to disappear from the American press reports as several new cases emerged which were more sensational. Alger Hiss, a much worse case, had already been indicted on the evidence of Whittaker Chambers who had also worked for *Time*, and there was a bitter fight going on around Owen Lattimore. So it left me with less and less real information about Pip.

In the meantime Eileen and I had moved to Paris, where there were already a dozen or more American exiles from

McCarthyism, mostly Hollywood screenwriters, directors and actors, and a few other victims like the great American photographer, Paul Strand. None of them knew Pip personally, and as far as I was concerned he had simply disappeared into the American McCarthyite mess.

CHAPTER

11

By now Europe was as deep in the cold war as America, so that American exiles in Paris were in almost as much difficulty as they had been at home. The problem didn't touch me, but my Hollywood friends in Paris had to organise themselves into an anonymous collective in order to survive. None of them had valid passports, and though the French tolerated them and gave them *droit de séjour*, they were not free of harassment, so that what work they would get had to be done under the counter, not only to avoid trouble with the French but to prevent their work being discovered by the Americans who had blacklisted them, and were still hunting them down.

That was the situation that Pip stepped into when he turned up in Paris.

I was living at the time in rue Monge and I spent my mornings writing in a café called Le Soleil d'Or, just across the Pont St Michel on the Ile de la Cité. It was mostly used by advocates from the Palais de Justice just around the corner, but there was also a businessman's ticker-tape machine under a glass dome which looked like something out of Zola – if they had had ticker-tapes in Zola's time. But it was a quiet, sunny place and I was left alone with my work over a coffee and vermouth, so that when Pip walked in on me out of the blue it was not only a surprise, but I felt as if we were playing out a scene from a French film.

'How did you find me?' I said after we had exchanged a curiously cautious greeting.

'Somebody or other told me you were in Paris and where you lived, so I dropped in and Eileen told me you'd be here.'

'But when did you get here? I mean in Europe?'

'A week ago.'

'Where from, for God's sake?'

'Canada.'

'You mean they actually let you out of the United States, just like that?'

'Not exactly.' So far everything Pip had said seemed rather reluctant, but then he relaxed a little. He said he had gone up to the busy border at Detroit and walked across the bridge to Windsor in Canada, undetected. His passport was still valid. Though the Attorney General's department had called it in he had refused to hand it over. 'But it'll run out in a month's time, and since I know they'll never renew it I thought I'd better get as far away as I could while I still had the chance.'

It was almost five years since I had last seen Pip, and almost a year since his last letter, so there was a considerable gap between the Pip that I had known and this one. He was a bruised scarecrow. His face seemed to have dried up, he had aged, and his once frank and light-minded eyes were filmed over now with an impersonal, sardonic sort of suspicion, as if, looking out on the world, he wasn't going to trust anything anymore.

As we sat down at one of the little marble-top tables I asked him where he was living and he said he had a room behind the Ecole des Beaux Arts. 'Six by four,' he said, 'with a Metro track under and a couple of leaking toilets over.'

I laughed, but Pip didn't even smile, and I knew that the old, relaxed Pip was no more. Even a few minutes with him told me that much.

'You don't happen to know a good cheap French lawyer, do you?' he asked me when I had ordered him a coffee.

'No. Why?'

'They tell me I'm going to need one to get a *permis de séjour* on my expiring passport.'

110

'You really think so?' I said, and told him that the other American exiles had devised a system with the French authorities which seemed to work. 'Why don't you talk to them?' I suggested.

He sipped his coffee. 'I don't want to get involved with Americans,' he said. 'There's sure to be some bastard among them who's reporting straight back to the FBI.'

'Not among this lot,' I said.

This time he laughed, not a light-hearted laugh but a dry little cough. 'Still the same old Kit,' he said. 'Loyal to his friends.'

'You bet,' I said as cheerfully as I could.

'Don't mind me,' he said. 'I'm still a bit prickly, but I'll get over it.'

'You look all right,' I told him.

'No, I don't. I look up to my ears in shit, which is how I feel.'

He asked me about Eileen and congratulated me on my infant son Dick whom Eileen had managed to show off to him.

'I suppose you want to know about Judy,' he said.

I told him I did, but I wasn't sure how to ask.

'Judy's marrying Terrada next month,' he told me.

'I knew she'd left you,' I said, 'but I didn't know it had gone that far.'

'She's got the quickest divorce ever recorded in New York State,' he said. 'She and the judge had a marvellous time skinning me of everything I had, including my son.'

'Why? What did they do with the boy?'

'With half a dozen newspapermen in court the judge had to make a loyal citizen of himself, so he told me that my presence near the boy at any time would make it impossible for him to be brought up as a good American. So I was refused access at any time, and now Judy's about to give the job to Terrada.'

'Judy always gets her pound of flesh,' I said.

'I didn't think she'd want that much,' Pip said grimly.

'Not the boy. But you never did like her, so you always expected the worst of her.'

'I didn't like or dislike her,' I protested. 'I always thought she was the wrong girl for you, that's all.'

'You always thought I was weak and stupid, didn't you?'

'No. Just wrong, Pip. You should have married Aimee,' I said.

'Oh, shut up,' he told me calmly.

'Sorry,' I said, 'but I mean it.'

I had been studying Pip, thinking about how to deal with him, and I decided that he needed to be jabbed rather than pitied; and I think he wanted it that way himself. But even with my jabs he would not talk about Aimee or Judy.

'That part of my life is over and done with,' he said, 'so I intend to forget it as soon as possible.'

'Okay. Okay. I won't mention it again,' I said. 'But what are you planning to do in Paris?'

'I don't know yet. I still have a little money that Judy didn't know about, and I've got a friendly aunt in Blois. But I'll have to find a job if I can. You don't happen to know of any, do you?'

'I'm not the best person to ask. I don't know many French people, not that kind.'

'I didn't mean the French, Kit. My French isn't that good. I meant with . . . with . . . Oh hell, I don't know who with. Europe used to be full of my friends so I'll find something.'

We left the Soleil d'Or and walked across the Pont. He stopped for a moment halfway and leaned on the parapet and looked across the quayside at Notre Dame. 'You know, Kit,' he said, 'when I was about thirteen my mother read *The Hunchback of Notre Dame* to me when I was lying in bed with jaundice. And every time I look at that pile I wonder how long it will take me to like it.'

'Does it matter?' I said. 'Do you have to like it?'

'I don't know. But there's something so oppressively French about it that I don't think I'm going to be too happy in Paris until I can walk into that damned place without feeling hopelessly depressed.'

'Oh hell, Pip, that sort of feeling won't last for ever,' I said.

'Maybe not. In any case,' he said simply, 'I know one thing for sure. I know now that I never want to see America again.'

'You'll get over that too,' I said roughly, pursuing my policy of toughness.

'I don't think so,' he said with so little feeling of regret or misery that I think I was shocked at the time. 'My America is stone dead, Kit. Or rather it's dying of the kind of vulgar insemination that I used to think was going to save it. But I was so damned wrong.'

I still wasn't sure how to interpret this quiet denunciation of the great multitude and the noble republic. Pip was too calm about it for me to dismiss it as understandable bitterness, so I decided to wait and see how he felt after a few weeks' sanctuary in the safety of Paris.

We walked on and I asked him home to lunch, but he said he didn't want to throw Eileen's housekeeping out of joint. 'Invite me to dinner when you've fixed it ahead with Eileen,' he said.

He was still the polite and considerate man so I took his address and phone number and watched him walking (loping) up the Boulevard St Michel. I noticed his clothes. Pip had always worn expensive and well-cut suits which he managed to crumple into his willowy shape. He still wore a good suit, but now it hung loose on him, and in appearance he seemed to have reverted to the wiry New England type, the kind who lived out their weather-beaten lives on the bleakest part of the Atlantic coastline with sea-worn faces. As I watched him go I was going to say to myself 'the poor bastard', but I changed my mind. There was nothing beaten about Pip.

He came to dinner two days later, and after he had made a fuss of our son Dick, who told him he had a bag of bones in his knees, he showed us the last photograph he had of little Lester. It was the picture of a solemn and even sullen little boy. Pip told Eileen that as they had left the courtroom after

113

the divorce, Judy had generously offered to send him a picture of little Lester every year on his birthday. 'So that I could keep in touch with him growing up.'

'I hope you kicked her in the shins,' Eileen said.

'Now . . . now . . .' Pip said drily.

'I thought you were putting that part of your life behind you,' I told him.

'Did I say that?'

'You did.'

'Then I was a bloody fool,' he said. But then he looked rather miserably at the picture of his son and suddenly tore it up before we could stop him. 'You're right, Kit. I have finished with all that.'

But he was in fairly good spirits and he still had a good appetite. He drank three pastis before dinner and four or five glasses of wine with dinner so that he was rather mellow when we sat down in our little salon for coffee. He had given us some of the details of the Senate hearings and of his subsequent fight to keep out of the clutches of a federal grand jury. But I had to leave him alone with Eileen for ten or fifteen minutes because Dick was incubating what turned out to be measles, and it was my turn to persuade him to go back to sleep. I knew when I came back into the room that Pip had been telling Eileen something that he would not tell me, but I didn't know whether it concerned Judy or Aimee. As it happened it was about Aimee.

What he *was* willing to tell me that night were his corrected theories on America's destiny. Remembering his old genius for 'what is', I had asked him what he thought would happen to the United States if it went on cutting down all opposition to its current conventions.

'I don't know any more what to anticipate,' he said. 'I only know what to regret.'

'There's always plenty to regret,' I suggested, 'but that doesn't explain what's happening.'

'It's a sterile situation,' he said, 'so nothing's happening.'

'I would have thought that the whole damn country was in ferment,' I argued.

114

'It's in ferment all right,' Pip said, 'but only because it's turning itself over to the moral judgments and social brutalities of a medieval peasantry who have absolutely no historical connection with America at all. None, except the ignorance and prejudices they brought with them – the bastards – and the primitive myths they have taught themselves about the Great Republic. They're dragon's teeth, Kit. They've learned to read and write and organise themselves into intolerant clans, so they consider themselves a miracle of liberty, when in fact they are little better than ideological fodder for the destruction of whatever is left of the original Republic.'

'My God,' I said. 'You sound as if you've abandoned the people you always said were the real stuff of America. All that noble refuse from the teeming shores.'

'I don't believe in them, and I don't even believe in me. And that's that!'

'In that case Terrada wins the argument,' I said incredulously. 'You've handed it over to him.'

'Of course I have,' he said. 'He's the perfect model of what I'm talking about. Didn't I always try to convince him and the others like him that they could be something else if they understood who they were? But I was so damned stupid, Kit, that I was blinded by my silly faith in the populace. As far as I'm concerned America stopped being America after the great migrations; after the arrival of all those huddled masses yearning to breathe free. They invented the myths, Kit, or rather the myths were invented for them.'

'I can't believe it,' I said. 'You're becoming bitter.'

'No I'm not!' he said angrily. 'I've recovered my mother wit, that's all. The only America I respect any more is damn near the original thirteen colonies, and maybe the first thirty years after the War of Independence.'

'It's the Prince talking,' I persisted. 'You're becoming a reactionary.'

'I'm becoming the American I was born to be,' he said rather sourly. 'And now by God I'm proud of it and the rest can go to hell.'

115

I had made allowances for the pastis and the wine, but I knew that Pip meant what he said. He had a way of speaking now that was as dry and as tough as he wanted to be.

'I'm sorry you've changed your mind,' I told him, 'because you had convinced me, years ago, that you were right. In fact I've always looked at America the way you taught me to.'

'Me too,' Eileen said.

'Then don't let me unteach you,' Pip said. 'You're not Americans, so the bastards can't get at you the way they got at me.' He leaned over and kissed Eileen and said it was time he went home.

He went off with a little bit of a stagger, but he had a look about him as if he was delighted to have shaken us a little. Why not? I think he was laughing at something when he walked home that night – if laughter is quite the word. But he was mocking something.

'He's so damned convincing,' Eileen said when he had gone and we were washing the dishes.

'I wonder why all Americans are so passionate about America,' I said. 'There must be something in the orange juice.'

'He told me about Aimee.'

'Oh?'

'Did you know that there had been a post-mortem which Judy ordered? She was sure Aimee must have been taking drugs, otherwise why else would she cut her wrists like that and smash the plates?'

'I don't believe it.'

'Oh, she wasn't taking drugs. But she was pregnant.'

'You mean that's why she committed suicide?'

'Nobody knows. According to Pip, her husband Jack said that if she was pregnant it was nothing to do with him. And she did leave a note, they found it, and it made a lot of trouble between Pip and Judy. It was the only note she left and it was addressed to Pip and said how sorry she was that she was doing what she was doing, but what else was there to do when the world was so rotten?'

'Why should that have made trouble between Pip and Judy?'

'Oh, Judy was sure that Pip had made her pregnant.'

'I'm not going to believe that either.'

'You don't have to believe it,' Eileen said. 'But Pip said he wished he had. He said he is sure that she didn't know she was pregnant; she would never have killed herself if she'd known. He said Aimee was a very moral girl and would have gone on suffering her own peculiar hell rather than kill an unborn child. He's sure she only wanted to kill herself. And he didn't think it was anything to do with remorse or sin or anything like that. He said she wanted to put an end to the kind of life that just wouldn't work for her, and being a practical girl she had done it as a practical thing. He thinks the plates must have been some sort of denunciation, but the real tragedy of it is, Kit, that Pip thinks it might have been different if he himself had had an inkling of what was happening to her.'

'What did he mean by that?'

'I don't know, but that's exactly what he said.'

I put down a large plate I was drying, and wondered if I would ever again be able to look at a plate without thinking of Aimee as I was thinking of her now. 'If Jack wasn't the father, nor Pip,' I said, 'I wonder what new kind of violation she had submitted herself to. She must have been pretty desperate, poor kid.'

We had already wept for Aimee so there was nothing more for us to say. In fact it was really Pip we began to speculate about. What had he meant when he said he wished he had been the father? Was it an offhand remark, or had Pip finally been hoping for something like that with Aimee? On the other hand perhaps he had been so preoccupied with his own troubles that he had never expected more of her than their old friendship. Was he regretting now that he had not made it more? Torn up his life and put it together again with Aimee on the other side of it?

We knew only one thing for certain. If it had been Aimee, Pip wouldn't be the lonely man he was now, loping like an old grey wolf up the Paris boulevards; trusting nobody; cutting himself off from the marvellous stuff he had once believed in; and not knowing where he was going or what his life amounted to.

12

We left Paris soon after Pip's arrival, and returned to London, so we didn't see what was happening to him day to day. But the next couple of years in Pip's life were, I suppose, years of sheer survival. He had enough money to last him only a few months, but he did get his *permis de séjour* after a long and complicated argument with the French and a wait of six months, which meant that he was in France illegally for about five months.

Nobody in authority was going to make it easy for this returned refuse from that other shore, and though Pip and the other émigrés did have loyal friends among Frenchmen in France, there was little that they could do in the face of real authority except protest when things got too bad for them. But they were better off in France than they would have been in Britain, where there was far less generosity toward these American refugees.

What I remember of Pip in those two or three years and into the fourth, were the brief meetings we had when we were passing through Paris, or when at one time we were living at Aix-en-Provence and he spent a week with us, shivering in our rented villa and cursing the brutally-clean mistral which cut the nuts off the chestnut trees with a freezing, frosty edge. Pip was too thin to survive the Provençal winter and he gave up and went back to his warm, damp room in Paris.

At first he didn't seem to fit in anywhere. He was trying to keep a low profile so that he didn't become hot American news when some newspapermen discovered that Phillip Lovell was now living in Paris without a passport. He couldn't find real work, and unlike the Hollywood exiles who got secret jobs on second-rate European and cheap American films made in Europe, there were no cheap journalistic jobs going.

At one time he lived by giving English lessons to the two boys of a French diplomat he had known in Washington, a small sinecure of generosity which was depressing and demoralising for him.

Then he got a job reading the American and British papers for an international press clipping agency which paid by the item cut. He told me that it was one of the most educative jobs he had ever had, since one day he would be cutting diplomatic news, the next day scandal, the following day heavy politics. It led him to another job, writing European film star scandal under an assumed name for a Hollywood film fan magazine. It was the first of his undercover journalistic jobs.

But it didn't last long because the Hollywood magazine found out who 'William S. Smiley' really was, and the assistant editor wrote him a sympathetic letter telling him they couldn't go on taking his material because Louella Parsons and her friends had enough influence to get the magazine shut down if they discovered that it was publishing reports from Phillip Lovell, alias William S. Smiley.

The first year was probably the worst and Pip went on shrivelling and ageing. Aristocracy, exile and poverty didn't mix with Pip. His disbelieving eyes were always looking out as if he dare not look in, and it was about this time, at the end of the first year, that he met a French girl called Monique Dreyfus.

Monique was a rather stocky, vigorous sort of girl, intelligent and tough, and rather catlike in her movements. She was fit and able, intellectually and physically, to deal with anybody who approached Pip with evil intent. It was Monique who held him up when sometimes he wanted to lie down and simply disappear. He was drinking a little too much, sometimes a lot, but Monique told him she was not going to tolerate that ridiculous American habit of getting drunk when in despair.

'You see it on the peectures,' she said. 'It's a silly, childish invention. You Americans just think you have to do it.'

Pip said that he would defend America at all costs, and he pointed out that the bistros of France were full of Frenchmen besotted with the drink of despair.

'So don't blame it on us,' he said.

'But it's the way you do it,' Monique insisted. 'You get to drink the way you get to religion. If you want to stay with me you can only get drunk when you are happy, not when you are miserable. I forbid it.'

Monique was a determined mother hen, but her strong voice, charming accent and Gallic logic silenced the willing Pip. Nonetheless he went on drinking a little too much, although I think he was actually saved that second year in Paris by alcohol, which blurred the worst edges of his predicament for him, and by Monique who preserved him until he was able to preserve himself.

Perhaps the real strength of Monique's influence was her contempt for everything that was happening in America, and her fury at Pip's sadness with the outcome. He ought to be glad, she said, because the misery he had suffered proved the barrenness of American behaviour. But in defending himself against her attacks Pip was often forced to defend America itself, which was good for him.

'If you have come to Europe to live, then you have to stop thinking about George Washington and Abraham Lincoln [Leencon],' she said one day when we were visiting them in the little flat she had just off the Marais.

'But I never think about them,' Pip protested.

'In that case you shouldn't be upset at anything that happens to you. You're on one side, and those *bâtards* in Washington are on the other. That's politics. But all that you Americans think of is what you are loyal to and what the other one is betraying, and it's all the same thing anyway – George Washington and Abraham Lincoln. It is childish.'

'It's the only history we've got, Monique,' Pip argued. 'So we have to live by the conventions of it. After all, every Frenchman considers himself the embodiment of the Revolution.'

They went on arguing, and we went on listening because we could see Pip coming to life. I think Monique knew exactly what she was doing. She was so marvellously normal, although her own upbringing was by no means normal. Her real parents had been taken away by the Nazis during the occupation and no trace of them had ever been found. She had been brought up by a French bourgeois family named St Jacques who doted on her as she doted on them, although they didn't approve of Pip. They thought him a waste of her French talent, her French future and her French respectability. But Monique, with her catlike fury and springy body, needed a challenge – something real and menacing. Pip's problem was real enough, but Monique was obviously delighted to take on the entire United States as well, and Eileen said it was because she must still remember the helplessness of the victim in the face of a huge and brutal Nazi authority. So she was belligerently at war with any other absolute authority which crushed the victim and rendered him helpless as well.

Otherwise she was a fairly conventional girl. She was a qualified pharmacist and worked in a white coat in a neat, glassy pharmacy owned by her adoptive father on Avenue Général Leclerc. Monique in her pharmacy was efficient and impersonal even with Pip, as I discovered one day when we called on her to take her out to lunch. I wouldn't have been surprised if, from behind her glass window, she had addressed Pip as Monsieur and asked him what she could do for him. She didn't like us making a personal call to her pharmacy, and she hurried us out as quickly as she could.

I thought for a while that in Monique Pip had found another powerful and dominating woman who would do to him what Judy had done – emasculate him. But that idea was dispelled whenever they began arguing, which was often enough, and I knew that this time Pip had found a challenger who put him on his mettle.

So he got through those first two years with some real help, and it was only in the third and fourth years that he began to find serious work, even though he was still forced to remain unseen and anonymous. I think it started with an agency man named Hughes. He was a Canadian working for one of the American feature services in Paris: an old hand who had known Pip in Washington and respected his unique kind of judgment. At the time the French were just beginning to cope with serious local resistance in Vietnam, so Hughes asked Pip to write a piece on the likely development of the situation. Using another *nom de guerre*, 'George Grenville', Pip predicted serious trouble for the French and possible disaster as the war with the guerrillas in Vietnam escalated.

'The French cannot win,' Pip wrote, 'nor can anyone seriously hope to conquer the Vietnamese. They have, in their history, defeated or absorbed at least eight foreign invasions and they have virtually been at war with foreigners or conquerors for almost five hundred years. Given the arms and the terrain and the national will, it will not be possible for the French to defeat the Vietnamese guerrillas because they simply melt into the countryside every time the French Army tries to do battle with them.'

It was a daring prediction at the time and the French didn't like it. But Hughes stuck by his man and his anonymity, and thereafter Pip was given other analyses to write, not only on Asian affairs but on French affairs, which he was now equipped to deal with. The curious thing about his anonymous journalism was that Pip had become much better at it than he used to be. What I detected in his writing now was a journalistic knife edge which he had always lacked. In fact it was the difference between a rather soft man and a very brittle and keen-edged one: the post-McCarthy Pip.

I don't know why Monique and Pip didn't get married, but it was probably Pip's status, or lack of it that bothered them. Without a passport he was nothing in French law, even though he held a French *permis de séjour*. In those days every one of these American exiles half-expected the long arm of the Washington committees to pluck them violently from their temporary safety and return them to the jurisdiction of the Federal courts, and I think it was Monique who didn't want to be the remnant left behind. She wasn't going to be a victim, even indirectly, of those American *salauds*.

So they settled into a sort of married life, living mostly in Monique's flat and taking a holiday from time to time in the Dordogne or in Brittany, but never on the Côte d'Azur which Monique considered effete and foreign and lacking in history. She knew Brittany very well and gave Pip long lessons, *sur place*, on the Vendée and the activities of the Chouans in 1793. She had a small 4 CV Renault, and the two or three times I rode with them I swore afterwards that I could never ride in the car with them again. They were both very bad drivers and they quarrelled constantly about the traffic, the *code de la route* and the mistakes one or the other was making turning left or right or swerving or stopping, etc. In fact Pip was becoming, under Monique's guidance, something of a Frenchman, and I knew that even if the situation in America changed and Pip somehow got a passport and could return to the States, Monique would not go with him. She would never leave France for long. It was Pip who would have to adapt himself, and there seemed to be a long life ahead of him living in a sort of twilight and never quite recovering his old identity.

Even so, Pip was more of a man than he had ever been, and when Eileen and I discussed them I couldn't help insisting that Monique was right. Let him forget his old identity, let him forget America, let him shrug off the difficulties of being virtually stateless and only half employed. To dwell on any one of these lost causes would only undermine his resolve; and even without any vast hope before him Pip somehow did have resolution and purpose in his life. Monique had made sure of that.

It was therefore a well-established Pip and Monique

whom we persuaded to spend a summer month with us in our rented villa on Cap Ferrat. It was quite an achievement, and it was one occasion which gave Pip the advantage because he was determined to come and he had to overcome Monique's stubborn distaste for the Côte and get her into the car and deliver her to our little house on the St Jean side of the Cap.

I may have given the impression here that his relationship with Monique was all challenge and fire. In fact it could be relaxed and happy, and it seemed to us that they were both in the best of spirits and when they came down to breakfast on their first day with us. It was a typical Midi day. It was June, the air was still, the sky azure blue, the sun warm without being hot, and we all felt the sort of postponement that those perfect days allowed us. No need to hurry or struggle or look out at the world. The sea was at the bottom of the slope, and an hour doing nothing over the breakfast table in the garden, with our feet on the dry dusty gravel, was not an hour wasted but an hour stored up. It was heaven.

'What in God's name do you do around here all day?' Pip asked me, flopping back in his chair, his head tilted to the morning sun.

'Work,' I said. 'In the mornings anyway.'

'Where? How?'

'Anywhere,' I said. 'On the beach, in the garden, any-where in the sun.'

'You should wear a hat,' Monique told Pip as she shaded his eyes with her two hands.

'I've never worn a hat in my life,' he said.

'Then you ought to wear one now. It's not good to have the sun beating down on your head like that. It affects the balance.'

'Get a white panama,' Eileen suggested. 'It'd suit you.'

'I'd look like a tobacco auctioneer,' Pip said.

'Oh no you wouldn't,' I told him. 'You'd look more like the British Colonial Office chap who advises the Governor of Sierra Leone to keep the natives off the streets.'

'I've given up advising governors,' Pip said. 'And publishers too, as it happens.'

Two days before their arrival we had read in the Paris edition of the *New York Herald Tribune* that the man who had been responsible for publishing Pip's books had been brought before the Senate subcommittee, and though a dozen other books were mentioned, the principal stigma for him was Pip's book and Pip himself who was supposed to have subversively influenced the publishing house as a 'special adviser'. Pip had not been mentioned for some time in any of the committee's activities, but even now the mention of his name was enough to condemn the man who had once published his books.

'I wonder if it will ever end,' Eileen said now in our sun-soaked lethargy.

'What?'

'All this McCarthy business.'

'Only after we've had another war,' Pip said.

'You really think there's going to be another war?'

'Sooner or later we'll start one up in Asia.'

'I can't see Americans fighting another war after Korea,' I said.

'That only goes to show how little you know about the United States. They'll not only fight another bloody war but they'll fight it with bloody passion and bloody conviction. Moreover they'll use everything they've got.'

'I don't believe it,' I said. 'They'll never use atomic weapons again. Too much against them.'

'If they have to use them they will,' Pip insisted. 'There's a whole generation of patriots who have to be beaten to pulp before they begin to discover what they're being patriotic for.'

'So who's going to beat them to pulp?'

'I don't know,' Pip said. 'But it'll be little men with slanty eyes.'

'You're too often right to argue with, but how many years hence will all this take place?' I asked him.

'How do I know? Ten, twenty, even thirty. America

126

moves on traumas, Kit. Only the next time when we get bogged down in Asia it'll become the sort of nightmare that'll tear the nation to pieces. After which we may finally get a generation that isn't afraid of the myths and the cults, and may even forget their peasant prejudices and maybe even change the emphasis.'

I held my breath. This was a little of Pip's old faith coming back, even though it wasn't the starving millions who were going to change the emphasis but a 'generation' unafraid of the myths and cults. It was a step in the old direction.

'I don't believe any of it,' Monique said. 'It will always be Washington and Lincoln with Americans, no matter what they do.'

'You don't have to believe any of it,' Pip said. 'All you have to do is wait and see.'

'Is that what you're doing?' I asked him.

'I guess so,' he said, and he told Monique that they ought to go, 'if you've had enough of this lotus-eating.'

'Where are you off to?'

'I don't know. Up the Corniche, or maybe we'll go into Nice. Monique has never seen Nice. Or Monaco. I want to go to the Prince's old Maritime Museum which I haven't seen since I was twelve years old. Don't worry, you two, we'll look after ourselves.'

'Are you coming back to lunch?' Eileen wanted to know.

'No. We'll be back this evening for dinner. So forget us in the meantime.'

They went off in their 4 CV Renault and we didn't see them until that evening. They went off like that every day for the next four or five days, and it was one morning when they had gone into Nice that Dora Delorme drove up and told us that she had Lester Terrada staying with her, just five minutes away in her villa among the pines on the Villefranche side of the Cap.

13

When Dora Delorme suggested the meeting between Pip and Terrada I suppose I felt that I had to protect Pip, and when she had gone I began once more to feel that there was something wrong about the whole idea.

'It won't do Pip any good,' I said to Eileen. 'So maybe I ought to ignore it.'

'You can't do that,' Eileen argued. 'Dora's quite right. It's Pip's decision. He can say No if he wants to.'

'But why spoil their holiday? He and Monique are obviously relaxed and they're having a damn good time away from it all.'

'They're never away from it all, Kit.'

'I still think there's something else behind it.'

'What, for instance?'

'How do I know. But Terrada isn't coming all the way down here just to see if he can say Hello to Pip.'

'So?'

'I think it's Judy. She's up to something.'

'Well, you know her better than I do.'

'That doesn't help.'

I was still in two minds about it when Pip and Monique came back from Nice. They were very happy. They had bought themselves cheap bamboo poles, little ready-made lengths of nylon line with floats on them, and packages of sea worms wrapped neatly in damp newspaper. They were both kidding and laughing, anticipating the fishy pleasure of sitting on the *rade* at Villefranche that evening and hauling in enough *poissons de soupe* to make a *soupe de poissons*, which Eileen would make superbly.

We had a very gay dinner, our children (we now had two) were being nice to us, and everything looked auspicious. It was all so auspicious and so happy, in fact, that more than ever I didn't want to spoil it.

'Leave it alone,' my protective half kept saying to me. 'Don't ruin it for them now.'

But I knew that there was something deeper than the joys of fishing that both these people needed, so I took Monique aside and told her what Dora Delorme had proposed. Monique's summery mood was demolished in a second. She didn't say anything at first, but then she burst out fiercely: 'Why do you ask me? Why not ask him?'

'I was thinking of you too,' I said lamely.

'Nobody thinks of me,' she said with rare self-pity. She had given so much to Pip and all she had been given back was a fragment of the man he really was – even now. I had never felt it so strongly as I did then, and I suddenly realised that there was still something missing in Pip, probably the unfinished remnant of his lost marriage.

'All right,' Monique said grimly after thinking about it. 'Let him go if he wants to.'

'Are you sure?'

'Of course I'm sure. But let him have his fishing first, then tell him.'

'Do you think he'll agree to see Terrada?' I asked her.

Monique shrugged like a Frenchwoman. 'I don't know,' she said irritably. 'How do I know?'

But she knew, and I was sure that she would even encourage it because she was the kind of girl who wanted Pip to face up to Terrada and Judy so that he could finish with them; so that she and Pip could get on with their own relationship and make something whole of it.

'All right,' I said. 'I shan't say anything until you come back tonight.'

Monique went off looking miserable, and I cursed Terrada – not so much for what he had done to Pip, but for what he might still do.

At midnight Pip and Monique came back from their fishing with one of my son's beach buckets full of *rouquiers*, *blaviers* and *rascasses* and when the others had gone to bed Pip and I sat in the kitchen drinking a bottle of Guinness he had brought with him from Paris. He was still gay. He said Mediterranean fish were like Mediterranean fishermen:

'Short, dark and stinking of iodine. Have you ever noticed,' he went on, 'how nature makes affinities between animal and man in primitive societies? Look at the Eskimo and the seals, the Red Indian and the buffalo, the Australian and the kangaroo.'

I let him finish the thought and then I told him about Terrada and Judy and his son, now almost thirteen years old, coming down to Dora Delorme's specially to see him.

Pip didn't catch his breath or show any sign of drama. He looked long and sadly at the empty Guinness bottle and said quite calmly: 'I knew the day would come sooner or later.'

'It doesn't have to come,' I said. 'You don't have to see them.'

He didn't hear me. 'Why do you think he wants to see me?' he asked.

'God knows,' I said.

'Do you think he wants to recant his denunciations and help restore me to my proper place in society?' Pip said cynically.

But I think he secretly meant it. As for Judy: who knows what emotional inventions his imagination was supplying him with about Judy.

'All right, Kit,' he said drily. 'It might be interesting.'

He went upstairs to bed then, but came down again five minutes later when I was locking up the garage and said: 'There's only one condition.'

I knew he had been talking to Monique. 'What's that?' I asked.

'You and Eileen must come along, and Monique as well.'

'What do you want us along for?'

Pip shrugged. 'I'd feel happier about it, that's all.'

But I guessed that it was Monique who wanted plenty of witnesses to whatever was said and whatever happened between them. Monique was ready to fight, but Monique was as nervous and as suspicious as I was.

So was Eileen when I told her Pip had agreed to see Terrada. 'If there's anything dirty behind all this I'll make Dora Delorme's life an absolute hell. I'll make her do something awful which will get her thrown out of France.'

It was already that kind of situation, so next day I arranged by phone with Dora that we would all go up there to dinner on the Friday, telling her that anything said by Terrada must be said in front of all of us.

'Lester won't like that, Kit,' Dora said. 'Nor will Judy.'

'It's that or nothing,' I told her.

'Oh, very well,' she said. 'It's a Friday, so I'll get a nice big *loup* [sea bass], and I'll prepare one of my famous mushroom sauces.'

This time I didn't feel so badly because our side seemed to have control of the situation. But I counted without Judy.

On the Friday morning we were all eating breakfast under our big bay tree when we heard Dora's car stop on the road outside and then drive off again. Then I saw Judy, with her son clinging to her arm, come determinedly up the gravel drive towards us. Monique had never seen her before but she knew instantly who it was, and we must have made a grim tableau as we watched her approach.

Judy had also changed. Like Pip she seemed to have shrunk. She looked almost mouselike. But there was something very determined in the way she walked up that path, eyes down, as if she wanted something and was going to get it. It must have taken some courage, although I think it almost failed her at the last moment.

'Hello, Kit,' she said nervously to me, as if I had to take the strain of this encounter, as I had once before.

'Hello, Judy,' I said.

131

I glanced at Pip, who was not at all sure what to do, or who to look at.

'Hello, Pip,' she said.

There was an awkward moment when they had to make up their minds whether to peck at each other's cheeks or shake hands or do nothing. They did nothing.

'Say hello to your father,' Judy said, trying to release herself from her son who still kept a very tight grip on her arm.

It seemed such a ridiculous and pathetic thing to say, particularly when the boy refused to respond, that I tried to fill the gaps of embarrassment by introducing Monique Dreyfus. Then we made a lot of fuss about getting extra chairs, and Eileen offered her coffee.

'I don't like French coffee,' Judy said. 'But I'll have a little.'

Why had she come here? We were all silently asking the same question, and I felt sorry for Pip who was trying to ask polite questions of health and well-being, and at the same time cope with the presence of his son. The boy simply clung to his mother until she said irritably to him (although she apologised to him later):

'Don't cling, Lester. Sit down on your own chair.'

I realised that it was time to leave them alone. In fact Eileen had gone into the kitchen on some excuse. But Monique sat determinedly still, and as I got up Pip said in a sudden panic. 'Don't go, Kit.'

'I did want to talk to you alone for a moment, Pip,' Judy told him.

'No!' Pip said nervously. 'It's a bit awkward.'

'But . . .'

It was Monique who couldn't stand any more of it. She leapt up and almost ran into the house. When I got up to follow her Pip said: 'If you go, Kit, I'll simply go with you.'

'All right, all right,' Judy said unhappily. 'It's nothing vital. All I wanted to say, Pip, is that Les has something important to tell you, and I simply wanted to ask you to . . . to be generous with him.'

132

'Generous?' I heard little strings snapping in Pip's nervous system. 'Generous about what?'

'Please try to understand him,' Judy said. 'That's all I'm asking.'

Pip's laugh sounded like a man defying pain. 'You can go to hell,' he said calmly.

Judy tightened her mouth. 'Then at least see him alone,' she begged. 'Not with everybody else.'

Pip shook his head. 'I can't risk that,' he said.

'Why not? It won't hurt you.'

'How do I know it won't?'

'I give you my word.'

I watched Pip dry up a little more. 'Is that supposed to be reassuring?' he said.

Judy pulled her son closer to her for a moment. 'All right,' she said. 'But Lester's not here to make trouble for you, Pip. Please don't think that.'

'Then he doesn't need to see me alone,' Pip said.

'But . . .'

'I'll see you with my friends, Judy, or not at all. That's as far as I'm going so why make such a fuss of it? As it is I'm being generous.'

'I think you're being unreasonable,' she snapped, unable to hide her resentment and her conviction in her old authority. 'It's the least you can do, and it isn't much.'

'Don't start telling me what to do,' Pip said, 'because I'm quite happy to call the whole thing off. So shut up, Judy, and watch your tongue.'

Judy took out a handkerchief and wiped her mouth firmly with a corner of it. She recovered herself and said, 'I'm sorry, Pip. I didn't mean to tell you what to do. I'm only trying to do the best for both of you.'

'You do what's best for Lester and I'll do what's best for me,' Pip said.

'All right, all right. I won't press it now. Do you want to talk to little Lester?'

'What do you expect me to say to him?' Pip almost snarled, but this time I saw the old haunted look return. Pip was still very vulnerable, particularly where his son was concerned. The boy was still clinging to his mother, head down, hating all this, refusing to look at his father or take any part in what was happening.

Judy gave a little shrug of pain and regret, and then Monique returned, after which there was nothing left but to get Judy back to Dora's villa.

'Could you drive me back?' she asked Pip.

Monique sat up and said, 'No he can't.'

'Please . . .'

'He has no French driving licence, and his *permis de séjour* is almost useless because he hasn't a valid passport,' Monique told her with considerable relish. 'If the police stopped him, what do you think would happen?'

Judy bit her faint bottom lip so I said I'd do it, and as I drove them home in the Renault Judy asked me about Monique.

'Who is she?'

'She's a French girl named Monique,' I said.

'Don't be cynical with me, Kit. I asked a perfectly civil question.'

'Sorry,' I said. 'But I'm damned sure Dora Delorme told you all about her.'

'Only what Dora knows, which isn't much. Are they married, or planning to get married?'

'You'll have to ask them that,' I said.

'Well at least you can tell me how long they've been together.'

'As far as I know they've known each other two or three years,' I told her. 'And that's all I'm going to tell you, Judy.'

'She looks awfully tough.'

'She's damned tough,' I said. 'And it's all on Pip's side.'

'I can see that,' Judy said.

She was being very disciplined and conversationally pleasant about it, as if I too had to be won over. But my barriers were almost as high as Pip's, except that I felt sorry for the boy who sat in the back seat of the Renault and listened attentively to every word we said, which inhibited

134

me. I didn't want to hurt the boy. But I did have to make my point with Judy.

'What are you up to?' I asked her as we went up over the hill and broke out on the Villefranche side.

'I'm not up to anything,' Judy said, 'so don't be rude.'

'There's something behind all this, Judy,' I said, 'and I want to be sure it isn't going to do Pip any damage.'

'You've got no right to say that,' she said angrily.

'Then what's your point in bringing Pip and Lester together again?'

'That's my business and Pip's and Lester's. Not yours. So don't interfere.'

'I'll interfere as much as I like,' I told her, angry myself.

Again she bit her lip, literally, to bite off every bitter word lying in wait for me. When she had won the little battle with herself she said, 'Please don't interfere, Kit. I don't like doing this, but I've got to. So I'm begging you not to interfere.'

'I'm not interfering,' I told her. 'I'm just watching out for Pip.'

We had arrived at Dora's front gate. I didn't want to go up the drive because I had no desire to run into Terrada. I didn't want the problem of deciding how to greet him, or whether to greet him at all.

Judy sat in the car for a moment and I waited, knowing that she had something to say.

'Pip's changed, hasn't he,' she said bitterly, as if Pip had failed to live up to some extraordinary expectation of him. 'Such a pity.'

I laughed and opened the back door for the boy to get out. I left them standing at the gate of Dora's villa and drove off without saying anything more.

I don't remember how we filled the rest of that day. I only remember how glad we were at 7.30 when we finally walked down to the Renault in the street wearing our best disguises. But as I opened the door of the little 4 CV Pip stood back.

'Sorry, Kit,' he said. 'But I don't think I can face it.'

'You aren't coming?' I said.

'No,' he said. 'The hell with it.'

I could smell pastis, and Pip's eyes were not quite focussed on what he was looking at, which was me.

Monique pulled his arm. 'You should not have been drinking,' she said. 'So come. You promised Dora you would come.'

'Well I'm unpromising her,' he said.

'What for? Why don't you come and get it over and done with.'

'Are you changing your mind?' Pip said irritably to her, the pastis filling the air now. 'You were telling me yesterday not to go. You were being so goddam French about it. *Jamais, jamais, jamais*, you said.'

'Well I'm telling you today to go and see what they're up to.'

'I know what they're up to,' Pip said. 'They want to inspect the ruin of the great Lovell of fame and fortune.' Pip laughed. 'But I'm not going to give them the old satisfaction.'

'You're drunk,' Monique said angrily.

'Maybe Lester wants to get down on his hands and knees and beg you to forgive him,' I suggested.

Pip hit the car roof. 'Damn good idea, Kit. So tell him to come over here and do it,' he said. 'I'm not going over there.'

'Well why don't you come and at least find out,' Monique said, appealing to him this time.

'Why should I even talk to the bastard? Why should I even be in the same room with him? *En avant, mes amis*.'

'Are you sure, Pip?' I said as Eileen got into the car.

'Damn sure,' Pip said. 'I'll walk down to the village and have a quiet meal all to myself.'

'All right,' I said. 'But what do you want me to tell Dora?'

'Nothing, for Christ's sake. Tell her that I changed my mind. That's all you have to tell her.'

'Just as you say.'

'You're disgusted, aren't you?' Pip said as I started the car.

136

'No! But I wonder what you would have been like if you hadn't taken that pastis,' I said.

In fact I felt sorry for Pip. I knew how much of his attitude was the result of the pastis, but I also knew that Judy and Terrada had undone him, and I could see already that he had to draw on all his resources to keep dignity, honour, resentment, anger, self-pity and revenge to manageable proportions. I drove off and left him standing in the street holding the villa's cat which he had plucked from the car bonnet.

We arrived at Dora's in gloomy silence and Terrada and Judy were sitting on the terrace waiting for him. When Pip didn't appear I could see them exchange worried looks, wanting information from each other.

'Where's Pip?' Dora called out as we walked up the drive.

'He changed his mind,' I said.

'Oh, the bastard,' Dora said calmly as if she had half-expected it.

I kept a solemn face but I laughed secretly as Terrada and I faced each other and failed to shake flabby hands. Dora, who had obviously stage-managed this moment on the terrace for their meeting, put one plump hand on Terrada's shoulder and said heavily:

'Never mind, Lester. There's still plenty of time.'

But I wondered.

Terrada was now a huge, tousled hulk of a man. He had a large furrowed face and thick hands, plump wrists and a crumpled shirt. He looked and behaved like a big political success, which surprised me because I had stupidly made the mistake of thinking he would be embarrassed to come face to face with anyone who was a close friend of his victim. But it didn't seem to register, because there was some sort of blind and massive barrier around him which nothing could penetrate.

'I remember you . . .' he said to me after a while, but he actually said it to the wall.

'I hope you do,' I managed to say.

Everything in that house was usually built around Dora,

who was moulded into her chair, but Terrada was now a rival. He didn't seem to see anyone in particular. He had troubled eyes that never acknowledged anyone, and his pronouncements were sent impersonally into space, as if there were someone far out there waiting for them. He filled a big chair with his crumpled bulk and began to be intelligent and clever about European politics, de Gaulle, Germany, the U.S. Fleet in the Mediterranean; all of it wrong.

But was that all?

I watched Monique and Judy because they watched each other, and I knew it was only a matter of time before one said something sinister to the other. It was Judy who began it.

'I suppose you persuaded Pip not to come,' she said to Monique.

Monique was holding a glass of vermouth in her hand, which was unusual for Monique, who didn't like drinking before or after dinner. She stopped rattling the ice in it for a moment and I had the crazy idea that she was about to throw the drink in Judy's face. But she surprised me because she said very calmly:

'Why should I do a silly thing like that?'

'Because you probably think you have to protect him from us.'

'Pip can protect himself,' Monique said. 'He doesn't need me to tell him what he can or can't do. He is not like that with me.'

'Why didn't he come then?'

'He didn't want to see you,' Monique said, and by remaining sweet and sour she was showing these Americans that she was not going to flatter them with a display of bad temper. But she couldn't quite keep the contempt out of her voice.

Then Judy surprised me. 'Couldn't you *please* talk to him,' she said mildly to Monique. 'Couldn't you at least persuade him to talk to Lester?'

I don't know whether it was Judy being a gentlewoman

138

or Judy asking a favour, but Monique didn't like it and she said irritably: 'Why ask me? I have already tried to persuade him to come here. I don't want him hiding from you and your big husband. If you all have something to settle among yourselves then I say to him settle it. So don't ask me to do any more than that. It's up to him. He's a man. . . .'

'Don't worry, Judy. There's lots of time,' Dora said again and I decided that so far Monique had had the best of the encounter because Judy got up and left us.

In fact she had really gone to get the living proof of what she had in hand, her son. The boy came out with his mother and went straight to Terrada and leaned against his knee. Terrada put a large affectionate hand gently on the boy's waist without really seeing him, while he went on pronouncing. Monique had stretched out her legs and was balancing her drink on her stomach and staring at the evening sky. But I think she was making up her mind to accept that sentimental challenge of the boy.

'It's not a healthy situation,' Terrada was saying.

He meant the situation in Italy. I read it as the situation here between fathers and mothers and sons and lovers. Fortunately Madame Lotta, Dora's cook, announced that the first course would be served in a few moments, so we sat around the big white table on the terrace and I heard Terrada telling the boy he must go to bed now, although it was quite clear he was not going to obey and was not expected to obey.

'Two first courses,' Dora said as we sat down, 'then my lovely big *loup*. It's this big.' She stretched out her hands to make a giant fish. A *loup* was the tastiest and the most expensive fish you could buy at the time, and the sort of fish you could cook fresh in ten minutes while the first course was being eaten.

We were halfway through the first two courses when Madame Lotta came out and asked her mistress where the big fish was.

'I left it on the icebox outside the kitchen,' Dora said.

'It's not there,' Madame Lotta told her.

Madame Lotta was ordered to look again. Finally Dora herself got up and looked. Then we all had to look for it, around the terrace, behind the kitchen, in the garden which was large and rambling and had no fence at all on one side. But the *loup* had gone.

'Those bloody cats,' Dora said.

'It was too big for a cat to steal,' Madame Lotta said, almost in tears.

'Human cats then,' Dora shouted mightily. 'They can see the icebox from that little path they use.'

It was clear that a villager had walked through the pine garden and had simply taken the *loup* with him. It was so ridiculous that we were all laughing, particularly Monique who was now proving herself equal to these sullen Americans. In fact it was Terrada and Judy who had lost the thread of the evening. They were the barren rocks upon which our little waves of silly fun and pleasure broke. We ignored them, and when Madame Lotta produced a huge plate of spaghetti we all considered it a huge success. The wine flowed, and the evening for the rest of us would have been saved if we were the reason for it. But we weren't, so all our pleasure was wasted.

That was how we left it, except that Dora said she was going to organise one of her 'awful' picnics for tomorrow. She said she had found a place halfway to Monte Carlo where nobody went, and you could even swim in the nude if you wanted to.

'So *please* get Pip to come,' she whispered to Monique in French. 'Please, Monique.'

'Don't concern yourself,' Monique said without looking at Judy. 'He'll be there this time.'

'It's a marvellous place. It's protected by prickly pears,' Dora shouted after us as we drove off into the night.

14

I think that Monique had decided by now that the Terrada family was more formidable than she had imagined, and now that she understood what she was up against she was going to make sure that Pip was delivered up to them, not as a sacrifice but as a riposte to Judy's offering of her son. Whatever they had made of him, before, this Pip was partly Monique's creation, and she was not going to admit weakness and allow Pip to hide himself away. Not this time. Now more than ever he had to come out into the open, unprotected, if only to justify her commitment to him and to show these Americans that she wasn't afraid for her handiwork.

So we four got into the Renault next morning and followed Dora's Peugeot to the overhung site, just outside Monaco. The prickly pears covering the hillside made it look less accessible than it was. I knew this place myself (as I knew all these little corners between St Jean and Menton) which disappointed Dora, although I wondered then how she had discovered it.

Judy and Terrada were not with Dora. They would follow later in their hired car with Madame Lotta to show them the way. But little Lester was with Dora, and I thought that was rather clever of Judy since everything now was plot and counterplot.

We unloaded Dora's Peugeot of the food, drinks, chairs, cushions and umbrellas and followed the path through the prickly pears down a rather dangerous slope to a lovely, shingly, rocky beach. But no sooner were we there than Monique took the fishing poles and removed herself from the rest of us in anticipation of Judy and Terrada's arrival. She wasn't going to stand over Pip.

Pip was left with the boy who had obviously been instructed to be polite and friendly. In fact he had a solemn sort of dignity which seemed to disconnect him from everything, not unlike Terrada.

'What's that?' he said abruptly to Pip.

Pip stiffened in amazement at this breach in the boy's silence. Little Lester was pointing to a pedalo a hundred yards out to sea.

'It's a thing you pedal like a bike,' Pip said. 'Water paddles . . .'

The boy withdrew, satisfied.

But Pip was not willing to let him get off so easily. 'Can you ride a bike?' he said.

'No, I can't,' the boy replied.

'Have you ever tried?' Pip asked rather aggressively.

'No.'

'Can you ride a horse then?'

'No.'

So far the boy had kept his temper and he was obviously being obedient. But the more Pip questioned little Lester the more I recognised big Lester, because I was sure that Terrada had never ridden a bicycle, and I knew he couldn't ride a horse.

'Can you swim?' Pip went on.

'A little.'

'What do you do then? Play tennis?'

'No. I can play chess.'

'Who do you play with?'

'My father. . . .'

Pip picked up a large stone and flung it violently into the sea near Monique. 'I'm your father,' he said to the boy.

'Yes, I know.'

'We haven't got much to say to each other, have we?' Pip said.

The boy shook his head and Pip got up. 'Well there's no use pushing it, is there?' he said and joined Eileen and Dora who were laying out the picnic. He asked Dora for a corkscrew. He opened a bottle of red wine and poured himself a glass and sipped at it as he walked around restlessly, looking at the roadway above. Little Lester was left alone and for the moment I was more interested in him than I was in Pip. He simply sat quite still on the shingle, an intransigent little boy waiting patiently for an ordeal to end.

It ended for him when we saw Terrada and Judy and Madame Lotta struggling down the slope. We had all managed it quite easily, but Terrada was in trouble. Judy had to hold his arm and guide his big steps, and when little Lester bounded up the hill to meet him Judy called out:

'No, Lessie. Keep away. Stay down there.'

The boy stopped. I stood next to Pip who was watching Terrada's slow and painful descent like a hypnotised bird watching the slow arrival of a dangerous cobra.

Finally Terrada was down, and with Judy still holding his arm he walked straight to Pip who was tossing a pebble from one hand to the other to keep both hands very occupied.

'Hello Pip,' Terrada said.

'Hello Lester,' Pip replied.

What else could they say? They did not shake hands. In fact Pip not only kept his hands occupied, he stood back a little.

Terrada was panting and sweating and he looked ill.

'I'll have to sit down,' he said to no one in particular and walked to a little rock and lowered himself onto it like a bear in a circus.

'It was a bit too much for him,' Judy said to Pip.

'So I see,' Pip said and turned away.

Dora called out to us then that lunch was ready. 'Can you make it, Lester?' she said.

'Yes, I'm all right,' he said and we all walked up to the picnic which was laid out perfectly on a check tablecloth with plates of chicken, cold meat, tomatoes, bread, cucumber, olives and four bottles of red wine.

'Monique. Come along,' Eileen called out.

'I'm still fishing,' Monique called back. 'I'll come when I'm ready.'

'Your cold chicken is getting cold,' Pip called out to her.

Monique ignored him, although it was obviously a cry for help. Pip was already ignoring Terrada who, once again, was inspiring pity and concern. I found myself worried for him and told myself not to be a bloody fool.

Dora and Eileen and Madame Lotta portioned out the chicken and the cold roast beef on plastic plates, put a tomato and a piece of cucumber on each one and handed out knives and forks and glasses. Dora said *'Bon appetit'*, and we all began to eat in silence since the only two conversationalists in this meeting would have to be Pip and Terrada.

But they went on eating without saying anything, and Dora had to start up some sort of conversation so she told us how she had found this place. 'I love prickly pears. I even put them in fruit salads,' she said, 'and I stopped on the hill one day to get some and realised I could get right down here with a little effort. So I came down and swam in the nude at midday when everybody else in France was at home eating their lunch.'

I couldn't help laughing. The picture of Dora, large and naked, plunging into the sea, was a natural comedy and Dora knew it and laughed with me. In fact we all laughed except the morose Terrada and the sullen Pip.

'I tell you,' Dora boomed. 'The local fish thought a new specimen of whale had arrived.'

It was good enough and we began to discuss the Midi, the tourists and the lengthening season, leaving Pip and Terrada to continue their dumb connection. It was, in fact, a fairly good picnic and when there was no more to eat Pip called out once more to Monique, as if he now knew what was about to happen. Monique ignored him, and Terrada got up and moved his body around behind us to sit down on the shingle next to Pip. I think Terrada surprised himself as

144

much as he surprised Pip and me when he blurted out in his big voice:

'I think it's time, Pip, that you and I agreed to talk.'

I saw Pip tighten his neck and his skinny back. 'Why?' Pip said. 'What have you and I got to talk about, Lester?'

Terrada took a deep magnificent breath. 'We ought to try to come to some sort of *modus vivendi*,' he said.

'Some sort of what?'

Terrada looked around at the rest of us as if it was very unfair that we should all be there when he didn't want us there. 'I mean some sort of moral compromise,' he said awkwardly. 'I'm sure you know what I mean.'

Pip gave a dry little laugh. 'D'you mean a moral compromise with my morals, or a moral compromise with yours?' he said.

Terrada plunged on determinedly. 'We've got to come to some sort of understanding of each other, Pip, so that we can go on living with ourselves.'

'I don't have any difficulty living with myself,' Pip told him. 'That must be your problem, not mine.'

Terrada didn't even hear him. He looked at the sky and he seemed to be addressing it. 'The trouble is that you and I misled each other years ago, Pip. That's the real cause of our troubles.'

'The real cause of our troubles, Lester, is you naming me before a Congressional committee as a subversive. So don't look any further than that.'

Terrada waved one of his big hands. 'We should never have pursued each other in public, Pip. That was our mistake.'

I was ready to explode myself when I heard that, but Pip kept his temper and even a grim sense of humour. 'Aren't you forgetting, Lester old man, that I didn't pursue you? You pursued me. Right into the ground. You buried me.'

Terrada looked surprised. 'Yes, but I think you ought to be able to see by now that it was part of the inevitability of it. That was the curse of the damned situation we were in. I couldn't help it. It was inevitable, Pip.'

This time Pip laughed. 'You're a bloody marvel,' he said.

Pip was quite sober, he hadn't touched more than a few glasses of wine, but he was being so casually derisive that I expected Terrada to show hurt and maybe temper. But Terrada was neither embarrassed nor upset. He was simply surprised that Pip couldn't see his point. 'You failed to understand America,' he said. 'You always refused to understand what was at stake.'

'Don't blame America for what you did to me, you bastard,' Pip said to him. 'In fact if I weren't a decent and loyal American full of the flag and faithful to the Constitution and the first ten amendments, I might have forgiven you for whatever you did to me. But you're a mujik Lester, and you'll never be anything else. . . . So always address me with cap in hand, and never be familiar with me under any circumstances.'

Once again I was amazed at Terrada's determined insensibility. 'I still feel that we should come to a moral understanding,' he persisted so that Pip was finally and hopelessly exasperated.

'All right! All right for Christ's sake!' Pip said. 'Let's come to your moral understanding. Only what particular sort would you like?'

'Would you agree to shake my hand and say it was not our fault and that our relationship is restored?'

Pip caught his breath this time, I heard it in his teeth. 'You want me to wipe it all out, is that right?'

'Yes,' Terrada said very simply.

'The whole experience?'

'Yes. All of it, if you'll agree.'

Pip put on his spectacles as if he needed to see better. 'There's only one way I could do that, Lester,' he said.

Terrada waited and I waited. Eileen waited and so did Dora and Judy. Even little Lester waited. He had been listening to every word.

'You'd have to announce yourself as a false witness, an informer,' Pip told him calmly. 'You'd have to recant everything you said.'

146

Terrada looked dumbfounded. 'But I can't do that,' he said.

'Why not?'

'Because it's unreal. I haven't the power to reverse the processes like that.'

'Then what do you want me to do?' Pip said scornfully. 'Reverse myself? Admit my guilt?'

'I just want you to wipe it out personally, Pip,' Terrada said desperately. 'Between you and me.'

Pip laughed and flopped back on the shingle as if he was finished with the conversation. 'The only way you and I could really settle this,' he said, 'is with the code duello. Then I could kill you and make a gentleman of you.' And Pip laughed again.

I'm not sure how Terrada would have pursued it if Monique had not arrived. She stood over all of us for a moment and looked disgustedly at the gargantuan remnants of our picnic. She picked up one wine bottle after the other but rejected them all.

'Haven't you any vin rosé, Dora?' she said.

'No, pet,' Dora said. 'I bought the best Chambertin and some very good claret.'

'You can't drink Chambertin and claret on a picnic,' Monique said angrily.

'I can,' Dora told her.

'Well, I can't,' Monique said. 'So if you haven't got any vin rosé, I'll go and make a fish soup. Kit! Give me the house keys.'

I gave them to her, and taking her bucket of fish she walked athletically up the slope like an angry cat. Halfway up she shouted at us: 'Nobody follow me. I'll find my way home on the bus.'

Pip had taken little notice of her. He was lying on his back with his face to the sun, trying to outlast the conversation. But Eileen prodded him and said, 'Hadn't you better go after Monique, Pip?'

'She's all right,' Pip said without getting up. 'She wants to be alone.'

147

'She's upset.'

'I know she's upset. That's why it's best to leave her alone.'

'Not this time,' Eileen insisted. 'Go on, Pip. Go after her.'

'Oh, for Christ's sake,' Pip said and scrambled to his feet and set off after Monique who had already reached the top of the slope.

Terrada watched him go. Then he looked at Judy for some sort of help. I don't know whether they exchanged a secret look or not, but Terrada picked up his espadrilles and hurried barefoot up the slope after Pip, stumbling awkwardly and shouting: 'Just a minute , Pip. I'll come with you.'

I watched them both hurry up the slope path through the prickly pears. Terrada had to stop to put his espadrilles on. He was awkward, almost helpless.

'Hadn't you better stop him?' I suggested to Judy.

'No,' she said. 'At least it'll spare him the inconsideration of having to talk to Pip in front of everybody else.'

'Please yourself,' I said and we watched them both disappear around a bend on the roadway.

Dora got up and put a fat arm around Judy, who was in tears. 'Les'll be all right,' she said. 'Don't worry. They'll be back.'

In fact they didn't come back at all, and Dora's awful picnic ended two hours later on my shoulders. I carried the chairs, boxes, umbrellas and fishing poles up the slope to the cars and we drove home in silence to find Monique sunbathing on the terrace. She said she had 'heetched-hiked' home.

'And where is he?' she demanded.

I said that Pip had gone up to look for her and that Terrada had followed, which meant that Pip and Terrada were now on their own at last.

Monique said in French: 'It's silly despair that makes the world go around, so why should I worry about him?'

15

We didn't start worrying about Pip until dinnertime, but even then we calculated that the two men were sitting in some bar or bistro going once more around the arena of their vast and bitter disagreement. We knew they were not at Dora's because she telephoned to ask if they were with us. Finally Dora arrived in her Peugeot with Judy who asked us if we had any news. It was about 10.30 p.m.

'No,' I said. 'Not a word.'

'Please Kit,' Judy said to me. 'Go out and look for them.'

'Look where?' I said. 'They could be sitting in one of a thousand bistros in Monte Carlo or Nice or God-knows-where.'

'Please,' she said.

It was Dora who pointed out that both men had been drinking wine at lunch and that if they took a little more to drink who knew what they would do, or what would happen. 'And, of course,' Dora said, 'think of the field day the American papers would have if those two were picked up drunk together. I can just see what they would do to Lester if it was ever discovered.'

Monique swore in French and said, 'If only God would become intelligent, it would happen.'

But Judy was very upset. 'Don't be cruel,' she said. 'It's unnecessary.'

Monique walked off in disgust saying, 'You let Pip alone. Don't touch him. If you do I'll denounce you.'

'Please, Kit,' Judy said again. 'Go and see if you can find them.'

149

'Listen Judy,' I told her. 'I don't care a damn about Lester and his reputation, so I'm not interested in rescuing him.'

'I wouldn't ask you to,' Judy said quietly, 'except that Lester is not very well, and he never could drink. Please, Kit.'

'Oh, all right,' I said. 'But it's a pretty slim chance.'

'I know. But you might save Lester some trouble if you do.'

There it was again, the victor expecting help from the victim.

'Don't you disappear as well,' Eileen called after me as I left. 'Bring them straight back.'

As I drove around Nice and Villefranche looking for them in bars and bistros I began to appreciate the responsibility they had put on Pip. I tried all the places I knew, and then I remembered Monique telling me in Paris that occasionally she would recover Pip from the Gare du Nord when he was drunk. He went there, he said, to catch the next train home to America. So I tried the little stations first and I found them sitting on the station platform at Villefranche, overlooking one of the most beautiful bays in the world, arguing drunkenly about the Pope.

It was midnight and when they saw me they said I would have to come with them. They were planning to catch the 12.30 from Menton to Marseilles, where they would catch the liner *Andrea Doria* home to New York.

'Wrong place, Kit,' Pip said, waving his arms angrily at the heavenly night of the mountain blue bay below us. 'Wrong place, ole man.'

'You're right,' I said. 'So let's get out of here.'

Terrada was a silent, heavy blob, but Pip was being active and aggressive.

'Got to go home, Kit, ole man. No place here for a loyal American like me.'

'That's right. So come on home now.'

Pip put his arm around me and said: 'Catching the twelve-o-thirty, any minute now. You'd better come along and make sure they don't play dirty tricks on me. They're full of tricks, Kit.'

'I know . . . I know all about that.'

'You don't know what you're talking about. You weren't there anyway.'

'No, but I'm here and it's time to go home.'

'None of that!' Pip said aggressively. 'You can't trick me.'

'I'm not trying to trick you, I'm trying to get you home. Monique is worried and so is Judy.'

'Hah hah!'

I could hear a train coming, an express which would obviously burst through the little station on its way to Nice and beyond. Pip didn't hear it but Terrada unpeeled himself from the wooden bench and staggered to the edge of the platform. I got a grip on him to hold him back, but he threw me off. I tried again and told Pip to help me.

'Let the bastard go,' Pip said. 'He's running away from Judy.'

Then Pip heard the train and began a serious effort to copy Terrada, heading for the edge of the platform. At one moment I held them both back and managed to keep a grip on them until the clattering old steam train shook and shuddered its way through the station. When it had gone I let them go.

'Can't go home now, Kit,' Pip said. 'Missed the damned ole train.'

'No, you haven't,' I said. 'There's another one tomorrow. You can get the one thirty-four to Marseilles tomorrow.'

'You're lying.'

'Come on home. It's late and I'm fed up.'

Terrada was now sound asleep leaning against the red stone wall which was thick with dry bougainvillaea in bloom.

'Don't go to sleep,' I said and held the swaying, jiggling, shuffling Pip while I contemplated Terrada. Then Pip raised a royal hand and pushed it hard against Terrada's heaving chest.

'You know only one thing that'll save this blue-piddled American, Kit?'

151

'Yes. Getting him back to Judy.'

'Only thing that's going to save this great American . . .' he was hammering on Terrada's massive chest '. . . is absolution. Total immersion absolution! But I can't give it to him, ole man. I just can't do it because I ain't the Pope. It's no good asking me. I told him I can't do it without a papal bull, and he said it wasn't necessary. But I can't give out dispensation, Kit,' he said painfully, 'no matter what he wants. I need a holy writ. . . .'

'Okay, we'll write to the Pope,' I said, 'only let's get Lester out of here because there's no train now till tomorrow.'

'Well I'll help you,' Pip said grandiosely. 'It's least I can do.'

In fact he pulled Terrada violently from the wall, got a grip on his shirt, shook him, tore the shirt and said, 'Sears Roebuck.' But together we got Terrada out of the station and into the front seat of the Renault without waking him more than twice. He woke up once more on the way home when Pip started singing *Deutschland Über Alles* and said it was the Bohemian national anthem.

'You can't deny it,' Terrada bellowed about something else. 'You just can't deny it.'

That was all. They were both asleep when I delivered Lester to a washed-out Judy who couldn't hold him up. I was going to help, but Dora got an arm under him and more or less lifted him into the house.

'I want to see you, Kit,' Judy said as I got back into the Renault. 'I want to explain something.'

'Nothing to explain,' I said. 'Lester's drunk, that's all.'

'But he doesn't usually drink, and I've got to explain something else. . . .'

At this point Pip pushed open the back door of the car and, seeing Judy, he jabbed a finger at her and said, 'Hah hah! He's gone, Judy, and you'll never see him again. He got the twelve-o-thirty to Chicago, and I'm telling you he said he never wants to see you again. He told me so, and I said that was damned cruel of him. So you'll never see him ever again, Judy. God took Lester away. . . .'

152

I pushed him back in and drove off before he could collect enough of his wits to get out again. In fact he was asleep once more when I arrived at 'L'Escapade' and it was comparatively easy, with Monique's help, to strip him of his shoes and trousers and turn him over into bed.

When I told her about the railway station Monique said: 'Some day he's actually going to get on a train and then he'll learn his lesson.'

Now she asked me if Pip had said anything. 'Did he say anything about his wife and her husband?'

'Not really,' I said. 'It was all drunk talk.'

'He didn't say what happened between him and Terrada?'

'Nothing intelligent,' I told her. 'You'll have to ask him yourself.'

'If he's given in to them, Kit, I'll keel him!' she said. 'I'll keel him.'

She refused to sleep in the bed with him. The smell of wine was disgust*ing*. 'I'll sleep in the children's room,' she said. In fact Eileen was already making up a spare bed for her in a corner of the children's room, and as we left Pip for the night he was smiling like a man with nothing on his mind but satisfaction and something very, very silly.

Downstairs, Eileen asked me what had happened, and I said 'Nothing' and hurried off to bed myself in case Eileen thought I was hiding something.

In fact I did not know what had passed between them, and next morning when Pip, like a broken stem, came down to breakfast I didn't ask. But Pip raised a cup of quivering coffee to his lips and said, 'How did you get us off that station, Kit?'

'You helped me drag Lester out into the car.'

'Did I fall down?'

'No.'

'Were you there?' he said to Monique.

'No, I wasn't, thank God. I was waiting here like a patient little American housewife.'

'Well, that's my memory of it too,' Pip said. 'I was just checking up.'

153

I wondered how much more Pip remembered. Quite a lot, I decided. But obviously Terrada remembered nothing at all because Judy came around at eleven o'clock to see Pip. She said they were leaving at three o'clock for Paris.

'It's too dangerous to keep him away from home any longer,' she said. 'Will you come and see him once more, Pip? I left him in bed. He's not very well.'

Pip shook his head.

'He doesn't remember last night.. He's not sure. . . . Did you settle it with him?'

I think Pip knew what he had said, or what he had not said, but he didn't let on now. 'Settle what?'

'Oh, please don't be like that. You know what's wrong with him, don't you?'

'Yes.'

'Then you can understand why he needs your friendship again, Pip. Be generous!'

I didn't know what she was talking about, but Pip did.

'I've been as generous as I can be,' Pip said, and he added with the enormous dignity of a headache and a hangover '. . . under the circumstances.'

'All right. All right,' Judy said. 'But just tell him you've forgiven him. I'm coming out in the open with it, Pip.'

'I've told him,' Pip said, 'that he needs a bigger absolution than I can give him. He needs a priest, Judy. Someone who can forgive him all his sins.'

'But he still doesn't believe he's wrong, Pip, so you can't expect him to change now.'

'Neither can I,' Pip said.

'In that case won't you try to accept that you and he see things differently, and that he had to do what he did?'

'*Merde* on that,' Pip said with his grey face.

'If you don't give him something back,' she said angrily, bitterly, 'you will be his real executioner.'

'Why don't you go away,' Monique said to her.

'Because I haven't finished,' Judy said.

We were sitting under our big bay tree listening to the morning chorus of cicadas buzzing their papery legs and rubbing their tinny wings. There was nothing left now but some final word from Pip.

'I'll see him off at the station,' was all Pip said, and Judy gripped his two hands for a moment before she left him.

I suppose I now dreaded that final farewell as much as everyone else did. But Pip seemed to prepare himself physically for it as if he had to give himself body courage to do what he had to do. He went for a walk alone, he took another cold shower, he dressed meticulously in a clean summer shirt and pressed linen trousers. He slept a little, and by the time we all left for the station he even managed to look lean and athletic. This time it was he who said to Monique that he would go alone, but she refused and insisted that we all go. I insisted too. So Pip shrugged and said, 'Okay. But don't interfere.'

'Then don't you make a fool of yourself,' Monique told him sharply.

At 3.20 we all gathered at Nice station under that tall cool roof and we looked like the Divers who had once gathered at the Gare du Nord to see Abe North off to America. We were there first, but a few minutes later Dora arrived with their luggage and porters. Then came the unathletic, sick, crumpled Terrada with Judy and little Lester. We stood around in an expectant and uncomfortable group waiting for the train to come in. You only had a few minutes to get on this particular train, so everything had to be said before it arrived.

Pip was being very cheerful and good-natured with the rest of us as if he had recovered something light-hearted in his life. But Terrada waited like a man who was about to accept some huge and difficult nomination. We all waited. Judy held little Lester tight by the arm so that he could not go to Terrada, and she spoke nervously with all of us in turn.

Then we heard the train.

At that moment Terrada was a few feet away from us and I heard Judy say to Pip in a suppressed voice: 'Please, Pip. Just a word.'

155

I could see all the old pressures working on Pip because the Terradas knew their man and they had him in the right place at the right time. Just a word, they said. What they were asking of Pip was his native generosity, his culture, his honour, his largesse, his modesty, his inclination to self-sacrifice, and his American sense of profound pity. I saw him going visibly through the lot, and above all through the very core of his upbringing. I sent him electric messages with my eyes: 'Don't let them get you now, Pip. Don't rescue them now for God's sake.'

But Pip didn't get my messages and I knew by the way his eyes drooped that they had finally got him with something inexplicable.

I turned away. I didn't want to see it or hear it.

But then Judy, guessing that she was about to win, made the mistake of making sure of it. 'You're doing the right thing,' she said to Pip. 'After all, Lester's got to go back to his kind of America, and he can't risk anything now.'

It was a fatal flaw, because I saw Pip dig in his freshly shaved chin as if his aristocratic athleticism meant something. And he said with a curious kind of relief, 'Someday, Judy, I'm going back to my kind of America, and what then?'

Judy waited for more. But there was no more. 'Is that all you can say?' she cried.

'Absolutely,' he said, and as if he could not trust himself to say anything more he turned to Terrada and said as crisply as he could manage: 'Goodbye, Lester. Goodbye, old man.'

The train was on us and Terrada turned in a daze towards it and climbed in without saying 'Goodbye' to the rest of us.

Judy's tears were splashing on the platform like sparrows' eggs, and Pip said in exactly the same voice: 'Goodbye, Judy. Goodbye, little Les.'

He kissed his son and helped him up the steps behind the luggage, and as Judy got in, the heavy door closed and the train was already moving. We caught a brief glimpse of them at the window, and I shall never forget those swollen

156

eyes of Terrada looking out helplessly over the vast and frightening horizon of nothingness.

'The poor bastard's dying of cancer,' Pip said. 'He's only got a few months to live.'

'My God, is that what it was all about?'

'Yes. But that doesn't make any difference, Kit. Does it?' he said. 'Does it?'

And I knew then what Pip had really come through. He had not only survived disgrace, misery and exile, he had come through the rifts and valleys of an appeal to the American heart, which is often the easiest route for anyone asking a man like Pip to betray himself. He had somehow survived even that, and I think he knew now that he had recovered the rest of his American dignity.

As for me – I looked admiringly at Pip and felt for the first time in a long long time that there was some hope for America after all.